# THE ADVENTURES OF SCARLET AND BRADSHAW, VOLUME 2

*The Apes of Devil's Island*

BY JOHN CUNNINGHAM

*The Darkness at Windon Manor*

BY MAX BRAND

*The Exploits of Beau Quicksilver*

BY FLORENCE M. PETTEE

*The Flying Legion*

BY GEORGE ALLAN ENGLAND

*The Golden Cat:*
*The Adventures of Peter the Brazen, Volume 3*

BY LORING BRENT

*The Opposing Venus: The Complete Cabalistic Cases*
*of Semi Dual, the Occult Detector*

BY J.U. GIESY AND JUNIUS B. SMITH

*The Radio Menace*

BY RALPH MILNE FARLEY

*The Sheriff of Tonto Town:*
*The Complete Tales of Sheriff Henry, Volume 2*

BY W.C. TUTTLE

*The Vengeance of the Wah Fu Tong:*
*The Complete Cases of Jigger Masters, Volume 1*

BY ANTHONY M. RUD

# THE RUBY OF
# SURATAN SINGH

THE ADVENTURES OF SCARLET AND BRADSHAW,
VOLUME 2

## THEODORE ROSCOE

ALTUS PRESS
2018

PUBLISHING HISTORY

"Moon Up" originally appeared in the October 12, 1929 issue of *Argosy* magazine (Vol. 207, No. 2). Copyright © 1929 by The Frank A. Munsey Company. Copyright renewed © 1956 and assigned to Steeger Properties, LLC. All rights reserved.

"The Blue Cat of Buddha" originally appeared in the March 22, 1930 issue of *Argosy* magazine (Vol. 211, No. 1). Copyright © 1930 by The Frank A. Munsey Company. Copyright renewed © 1957 and assigned to Steeger Properties, LLC. All rights reserved.

"The Little Gold Dove of Gojjam" originally appeared in the June 21, 1930 issue of *Argosy* magazine (Vol. 213, No. 2). Copyright © 1930 by The Frank A. Munsey Company. Copyright renewed © 1957 and assigned to Steeger Properties, LLC. All rights reserved.

"Claws" originally appeared in the July 1930 issue of *Action Stories* magazine (Vol. 9, No. 11). Copyright © 1930 by Fiction House.

"The Ruby of Suratan Singh" originally appeared in the July 21, 1930 issue of *Argosy* magazine (Vol. 213, No. 5). Copyright © 1930 by The Frank A. Munsey Company. Copyright renewed © 1957 and assigned to Steeger Properties, LLC. All rights reserved.

"The Phantom Buddha" originally appeared in the December 1930 issue of *Far East Adventure Stories* magazine (Vol. 1, No. 4). Copyright © 1930 by Fiction Publishers.

THANKS TO

Everard P. Digges LaTouche and Gerd Pircher

# TABLE OF CONTENTS

# MOON UP

*Under the night-witchery of the moon in a weird
valley of old India, anything can happen—and does*

# PROLOGUE

**MOONLIGHT. TO THIS** day it brings the narcotic, heady scent of jungle flowers and green river to my nostrils; chases a cold chill down to the pit of my stomach; and conjures in my mind the vision of Dr. Habighorst as I saw him first—a quaint gnome trudging a kobold's trail; and as I saw him last—milted to a pair of eerie eyes a-glitter in the moonray.

Weird, unpleasant memories, these; especially the picture of those bodyless optics shining like miniature moons in the moonlight on the sand, while the echo of desperate screaming still lingered among the black crags across the green river. Those bodyless glass disks—all that was left of Gulick Habighorst and his unknown assailant.

You may wonder, in reading, at the ready part I played in this bizarre story. You may believe me to have been ingenuous, or unwitting. Read through to the end, then, and recall your own shortcomings. Remember, too, the setting—Asia; India; the Orient. The very cradle of things strange. Have you ever caught the inscrutable stare of a Hindu fakir's eye, or known the subtly mysterious taste of a mango? There is a magic atmosphere east of De Lesseps's Canal impossible to Denver, Detroit or Old Broadway. And those of you who have succumbed to legerdemain in the fairly rational atmosphere of Denver, Detroit or Broadway can imagine me in that thoroughly irrational, Orient-steeped valley of Houglan Ra.

As for the moon: go out into your sane American back yard

any clement night, and see how irrational and improbable and ethereal she seems, somehow a phenomenon not to be taken for granted. The sun is friendly, wholehearted, masculine. The moon is aloof, feminine. Being a woman, she is given to subtleties. She is difficult to divine, illogical, possessed of a mysterious secretive way. Always she casts a spell. And when she dwells East of Suez, her powers are doubled. She's a little nearer earth out there. Aren't these lines from "Othello"?

> It is the very error of the moon;
> She comes more nearer Earth than she was wont,
> And makes men mad!

This is an East-of-Suez story. A story about moonlight and men made mad.

## CHAPTER I

# NIGHT VISITOR

CERTAINLY THAT VALLEY of Houglan Ra lay under the spell of the East. You have heard the phrase, "spell of the East"? Yes; it came from that jungle-infested little ravine sliced out of the Himalaya foothills to allow a crooked river to come sneaking down from the peaks. The valley of Houglan Ra. Oriental witchery simmered there between those clay-colored cliffs, and it was a place where no Christian man belonged.

There was a little and ancient Buddhist shrine squatting among the banyans of the valley's upper end, and when the hot breeze stirred its temple bell the valley was beyond relief. The bell emphasized the quiet, and the valley of Houglan Ra was too quiet to be healthy.

I sat on the bungalow veranda, sipping gin slings and listening to the silence. It occurred to me that the valley was always listening for something, too. There was no noise. Leaves rustled on the stalwart branches of the giant peepul tree commanding the center of the compound. The jungle that screened us in was whispering. Somewhere off a tiger coughed in its striped throat and startled a bevy of sleepy parrakeets into squeaking. But there wasn't any noise.

Mardo, my Punjabi native boy, squatted on his hams atop the veranda step and murmured out his evening devotionals. "Ram, ram, ram, ram, ram, ram—" But the prayer was scarcely audible; wasn't a sound. It fitted in, like the whisper of the peepul blossoms, the tinkle of the temple bell, the throaty cough of the tiger. It "belonged." But it made me nervous as I stared across the compound into an old-rose twilight that made a pattern of shadows among the cottonwoods and palms. I shouted at him to stop, and, naturally, he didn't. "Ram, ram, ram, ram, ram, ram—"

There was a monkey in the bungalow, and she began to cheep uneasily. The bungalow belonged to Holmes Bradshaw. You have heard of Holmes Bradshaw, the gaunt Kelantan naturalist. As a collector his name is known from Khartum to the Celebes Seas. It was he who donated the American Museum of Natural History its famous aardvark *(Orycteropus capensis)*; donated the Berlin Hall of Science its sole specimen of the rare climbing fish *(Anabas scandens)*; and donated Port-Light Pete Wong, the famous China Coast renegade, a bullet in the belly.

Early that summer I had encountered him in Bombay, and the usual libationary rituals of old-time college mates meeting ten years later in an out-of-the-way corner of the world were indulged. After a round of Scotch and sodas, he had dug into his pocket and handed me a key. Did I want to do some real hunting, some tiger shooting in a corner of the Orient that was one hundred per cent Orient? The key opened his bungalow up there. His house boys would take care of me; I would find a rack of guns; and there were tigers and plenty of game.

In a few weeks or so he would follow me and we could shoot together. He wanted to trek a river up there and shoot a few giant gavials to send the Jardin des Plantes in Paris. There were

*Was he the victim of
imagination, or did
he see watching eyes?*

gavials in that river measuring twenty-two feet in length; and
if I didn't get myself a prize crocodile hide and a few choice
tiger skins, he didn't know the place.

That had been some two months past, and Bradshaw had
failed to show up. Frankly, I was a bit dismayed at staying there
alone. I hadn't bagged my tiger, and I was going a bit deaf from
quinine. Houglan Ra was a lonely cranny of the world with
that temple bell tinkling softly into the jungly stillness and
Mardo squatting like a wraith in the evening dusk, murmuring
his prayer to Rama, the seventh incarnation of Vishnu, ruler of
Hindustan. "Ram, ram, ram, ram, ram, ram—" A devout chap,
Mardo.

**"SAHIB,"** Mardo spoke suddenly, "some one is coming. Footsteps come up the trail from the south."

That was Mardo. I tell you, there were times when the skinny
Hindu made my flesh crawl. Here he had been squatting on
the edge of the veranda, wrapped in a spiritual lethargy, eyes as
vacant as the soul of a brass image. Then suddenly he could
pivot on his heels, grin at me with a mouth made crimson by
betelnut juice, and proffer the information that some one was
coming up the trail.

Undoubtedly he had caught a sound foreign to the jungle quietude. No use in asking him how he heard such things, though. He would not admit he had heard. He would tell you he felt it, in his finger tips. He was a son of those jungle-clad foothills, and he often told me how the spirits of the night communicated with him.

"An enemy of mine in Peshawar has voted me a curse in his shrine tonight, *sahib*. It has dealt me the colic. Would the infinitely kind *sahib* loan me a drink of his whisky to ease the pain?"

Or: "Ah, *sahib*, the night wind brings me evil news. My aged mother in Calcutta died five minutes ago. Would the genial *sahib*—a gentleman and a prince, by the Oath of the Cow—loan me a few pice with which to condone the gods and salve her departed soul?"

Amazingly enough, in the latter case I found out later that his mother had died on the night in question. Perhaps there was something in the rascal's dirty finger tips after all.

Now he pointed a crooked thumb at the trail where it twisted atop the crest of a black sand cliff behind a wedge of palms, then ducked down through the trees and wandered up to the compound gate.

"Watch there, *sahib*. Soon you will see our visitor. No doubt it is the Bradshaw *sahib* whose coming you have awaited. Or would the *sahib* desire me to bring him his rifle?"

Damn the beggar, why should I need my rifle? As a matter of fact, I did have my trusty Maynard close at hand, but I wasn't going to make any show of nerves before that betelnut-munching scarecrow. However, I stared at the ledge of rock where any traveler of the trail would first appear, and watched; hoping it would be Bradshaw come at last. Mardo edged a little closer, and kept pointed thumb. "Soon he will be seen, *sahib*. He travels fast and has come a long way. He travels alone."

It wasn't Bradshaw, then. The naturalist trekked along with a squad of ragamuffins to tote his specimens and outfit. Who could it be? Houglan Ra was a neck of the woods particularly avoided by wayfarers.

Mardo finally spat a red sluice of juice at a lizard on the step and declared the man coming up the trail was not a native. A hillman wouldn't make so much noise. He rattled off Hindee jargon in his prominent Adam's apple, offering the hope that the newcomer would not bring evil upon us. A comfortable sort of fellow to have around, Mardo was.

I watched the trail and Mardo watched the trail. Night came rolling down from the mountain behind us and drank up the twilight at a gulp. The jungle folk responded by a roundelay of tooting bird-calls, squeaking trees and whisperings down by the river. It was dark as a whale hole across the compound, but a scatter of hot tropic stars promptly flashed in the sky, and directly behind the cliff where the trail would be walked a brilliant orange-hued slice of moon pushed into the sky. A moment later and the figure of our traveler was picked in outline against the shoulder of moon like a silhouette upon a screen.

"He is a stranger, *sahib*. We have never seen him before."

**TRUE** enough, we had never seen him before. At least, I hadn't.

From the veranda this nocturnal traveler gave the appearance of a Santa Claus flitting past the moon. The black silhouette against the yellow screen was that of a tiny figure almost bent double under a tremendous bulbous pack strapped on its back. A long, crooked staff supported and abetted a pair of spidery legs bowed as those of a parrot.

When the figure turned atop the cliff to start the descent of the path, it resembled nothing so much as some queer top-heavy jungle bird—a dodo marching out of its extinct past to pay Houglan Ra a visit. The dodo stopped against the moon for a brief instant, raised its staff, and hallooed:

"Hello, there, below! In the bungalow! Glad to see you are home!"

Mardo had a lantern going, and the shafts of light struggled through a glass chimney plastered with bugs, to add illumination to the compound which had been faintly lighted by the coming of the moon. The dodo atop the cliff had plunged out of sight, and it was not long before it came waddling out of the palms and up to the gate and across the compound. Now I saw it was not a dodo bird; it was a gnome. It puffed forward into the area of saffron lamplight, and from the shadows of the veranda I stared in rude astonishment. Gnomes, I had imagined, departed from one's world after one attained the age of ten. But this was Houglan Ra.

It was the huge pack that made him seem so small. Even so, he could not have stood over four and a half feet with his legs straightened. Amazingly skinny and bowed legs they were, arched under a round belly and ending in enormous, bare feet. Their owner slung the sack from his shoulder when he reached the veranda step, and straightened up with a ponderous sigh; leaned on his crooked staff. His hands on the staff were clutching twigs, and nothing but a gnome could have owned such enormous and wholly monumental whiskers. Like a miniature, foaming Niagara, that white beard fell in a cataract from the lower part of his face to the broad and huge-buckled belt strapping his belly. Yes, he was a gnome, for his bald head was made of burnished copper. But his eyes weren't really twin yellow moons, I guess. They were huge, dollar-round glasses simply reflecting the glow from the lantern in Mardo's soiled hand.

Well, he certainly was a queer apparition to pop out of the Houglan Ra darkness at one. I had to cast back in my mind to recall what I had eaten for dinner before I could believe this stranger had really come. I stared at him and his glassy, shining moons stared at me; and Mardo's Adam's apple had begun to mumble again. I couldn't find anything suitable to say besides "damn" and "what the hell!"; so the Niagara-like whiskers spoke first.

"Well, my friend," they said in a gentle voice that could only have come from a philosopher, "I've come a long, long way to visit you. Houglan Ra is a devil of a place, isn't it? I had the very dickens of a time keeping on the trail. The very dickens of a time. And if it hadn't been for the *moon*—ah, my friend, the *moon!*"

When he said, "the moon," he chuckled merrily, and rubbed his palms together so that they whispered. (So that was who he was! The Man in the Moon!) He went on:

"It's a wonderful phenomenon out here, isn't it? Brighter, more salient here than in any other locale of the world. I have been computing—but first, my friend, may I count on a little of your hospitality? I am very hungry and a finger of rum would not displease my dusted throat. I know you will pardon this rude intrusion on your solitude, and I am equally confident that my visit here will not prove amiss."

He chuckled quietly. "It may prove a good deal of a surprise, but— First, let me admit I know you; though you, possibly, have no acquaintance with me. As a former New York broker and money baron"—his voice was quite indulgent—"it is not improbable that you have never encountered my volumes, 'Atomology and the Proton,' 'Satellites and Molecular Activity,' 'Conceptions of the L-Ray,' and 'Lunar Electrolysis.' Works, I confess, a bit recondite for the lay mind. However, of these things we may talk later. At present I will foist myself on the more immediate gestures of your hospitality. I take the liberty of doing so because I know you will aid me, Mister Reven Staffard."

**WELL**, I could have been knocked over with a peacock feather. A dodo mysteriously appears against the moon, changes into a gnome, and marches into camp to inform me it knows my former business and present name. He must have seen my face, for he clucked appreciatively in his beard.

I couldn't get a single word out of my neck as he calmly stepped to the veranda, waved to the gurgling Mardo and asked to have his bundle deposited within the bungalow. When he turned on me again his whiskers were parted to show a smile. The moonlight got into his optics as he stood there, and his copper bald spot gleamed. Suddenly he pushed his face close to mine; fastened a twig on my sleeve.

"I," he declared in a hoarse whisper, "am Dr. Gulick Habighorst." His tone dropped an octave lower, and the words that hissed from his hoary whiskers stung the ear. "Reven Staffard, my coming here may place you in great danger. I carry in my pack a secret of inestimable value. Governments would totter and crash to own it. The pauper holding it would be thrice a king. The king without it could be reduced to ashes—to less than ashes. It is beyond price, wholly beyond human understanding. I, myself, fail at present to fully comprehend. But the peril—you will not mind. You will be richly rewarded. Reven Staffard," his voice was a husky echo like the sound of withered cornstalks rustled by an arid wind, "I am going to show you the most amazing, most astounding miracle of all God's world!"

CHAPTER II

# THE DOCTOR'S SECRET

**WHAT WOULD YOU** have thought? So did I. No doubt there were asylums for the insane in India as elsewhere, and if inmates could escape from them elsewhere they could escape from them in India. I glared at Dr. Gulick Habighorst and my mouth hung wide open and two moths flew into it. Mardo never moved a muscle to reach for Dr. Gulick Habighorst's ponderous pack; and the good doctor stood smiling with the moonshine glowing on his glasses.

Out across the compound a pair of monkies chattered in the peepul tree. The yellow moon rode clear from behind the black cliff and shed a spectral, algid ray into the cottonwoods. Somewhere up the crag a jackal started mournful ululation, and the perfume-freighted breeze from the river carried the gentle tinkle of a shrine bell to remind me this was the valley of Houglan Ra. In that case, Dr. Gulick Habighorst's words could be excused.

I thought them over as I spat and fingered the insects out of my mouth. Believe me, that unexpected speech from this be-whiskered old gnome with the Santa Claus pack was no ordinary oration. I had expected a nimble sales talk about the un-excelled values of the pots or pans or books or vacuum cleaners or safety razors he must certainly be carrying in his bundle.

His deft mention of "Lunar Electrolysis," "Atomology," "Molecules" or whatever it was had robbed the breath out of my lungs and set a stone on my tongue. Then to have him glibly recite my name and coolly announce impending perils and a miracle that could totter the world—no, it was too much for the same evening. I closed my eyes, opened them again, and was astonished beyond measure to see him still there.

"Mr. Staffard," he said gently, "I fear my words have more than startled you. Let us go into the bungalow where I can more fully explain and you can more easily understand. It would be better to talk in there. I promise you, sir, you will never regret this unexpected visit of mine. Never. And you are vastly fortunate that I place confidence in you. I might say that I did take the liberty of ascertaining something of your past from Lloyds, and Macklin's Business Bureau, when I was in Calcutta. Sheer chance, you see, has thrown you into this, and I am glad it is you and not some less meritorious man. All records have shown you a gentleman of unquestionable integrity. A man of no little moral stamina, I should judge, from the way you cleared that oil corner in the Wall Street exchange a few years ago. Come, then. May we go into the bungalow?"

Macklin's Business Bureau. Wall Street. Corner in oil. Mighty queer words to hear spoken in a God-forgotten place like that valley of Houglan Ra! A million times queerer, coming so unexpectedly from the beard of that totally strange, bow-legged, goggle-eyed little man who had, it seemed, just stepped out of the moon. The palms of my hands gave an uncanny little prickle as I fumbled to untangle his words. He, in turn, chuckled cheerfully, swung his pack to back and calmly stepped into the bungalow.

He wanted, he announced, a bowl of rice and some wine or rum if there was any about. And before he opened his pack, would I be kind enough to lock the door, draw the blinds, and station Mardo with rifle in hand to guard the keyhole?

So I yelled to Bradshaw's house boys, ordering food. You can imagine I didn't have much time to think things over. For some reason I complied with his demands, when I wasn't gawping at him like a high school sophomore confronted for the first time by a new physics professor with a cock eye.

It wasn't so much like the Orient inside the bungalow, though, or I never would have believed the visit at all. And Mardo did not stand at the keyhole with a rifle in his fist. If something was going to happen I wanted to be the gentleman

holding the shooting iron. Truth to tell, I didn't know but what
Mephistopheles himself might step in a cloud of pink smoke
out of the old man's opened bag.

**HE MADE** a queer picture hunched over a plate of curry and
rice, with a fresh wine stain marking the corners of his mouth,
and the light from the suspended ceiling lamp burnishing the
top of his hairless head. Mardo stood stiff as bamboo at the
door, and never took his eyes off the little old man. I repeat, I
stood planted near the sack deposited in a corner; Maynard
rifle resting in the crotch of my arm.

For some moments the old man did nothing but gobble food.
His mouth, like his feet, proved enormous, and he moved his
hands with an admirable celerity. Bradshaw's house boys had
almost hopped out of their unsanitary skins on seeing my visitor,
and I knew they had departed jungleward. But I was not thinking about them. I was thinking about Dr. Gulick Habighorst
and the astounding world-shaker he claimed to have in his
sack.

Pipe in mouth, he finally swung away from the table; knelt
over his bundle and fumbled with the strings. Yes, the door was
locked, I promised him, and the rattan blinds all drawn. Nodding
and smiling, he worked his twig-like hands into the mysterious
depths of his pack. Watching, I recalled his words: "I carry in
my pack a secret of inestimable value," and held my gun a little
tighter.

Fancy my reaction when he extracted from his sack the most
innocent object in the universe. I could have shouted with
laughter. Was this his secret? Was this the most amazing miracle
in all God's world! He fumbled it out of that pack, you understand, and placed it carefully on the table beside his emptied
rice bowl. It was a little wicker cage; and in the cage sat a little
yellow canary. The canary twittered, and Dr. Gulick Habighorst
stared at me solemnly.

He cleared his throat with vast deliberation. "I," he promised
me, "am without a shadow of doubt the world's greatest lunar-

ian." He poked a bony finger at the canary; began somberly: "The moon, my friend, has a great deal to do with the business in hand. Before I go further it might be well for me to explain the part you can play.

"Ah, my friend, you can play the part of one who succors a science without friends or backing. You have the money, but your financial aid will be as nothing to the honor, power you will gain.

"Again, you chance to be located in a position where I must of necessity ask your coöperation. In short, you have come to the valley of Houglan Ra; and the valley of Houglan Ra is the most potent locale for my experiments.

"I must work here. Those who live here must sanction and abet me. For it is in this valley, my friend, that one finds the strongest moonlight, the most powerful L-Rays in the world. Moonlight in India is unadulterated, the rays reflected proving a more, pristine saliency than elsewhere on the globe. To put it simply, the moonlight is brighter here than anywhere else, and brightest of all in Houglan Ra.

"It was in this valley some ten years ago I first discovered my famous L-Ray. Ah, the conditions were perfect—the rays salient. But you know of the strength of moonlight in India. Surely you have heard of folk here becoming moon-struck, succumbing to total lunacy from sleeping out under the satellite?"

YES, I HAD heard of folk in India becoming moon-struck; and I was by no means certain I was not witnessing an exemplary case of the same.

The doctor talked on, giving me no chance to interrupt. Bustling over to his sack, he dug into the bag once more, rummaged around, and drew to light something that gave me a real surprise—a lens. A large, round lens that might have come from the eye of some monstrous telescope. Surely that sack of the little man was proving a veritable Pandora's Box. First it yielded a silly little canary in a wicker cage; now a huge lens that must have been five inches thick and four feet in circumference.

Reverently my astonishing little visitor placed the lens on the table beside the canary cage. Then he squatted on his chair and talked.

I cannot here set down the speech that flowed from the man's prolific beard. I only know I began to listen. Mardo listened, too. The scrawny Hindu could not possibly have understood the import of the doctor's words, but he listened just the same.

One couldn't help but listen, for that queer little dwarf with the long, long beard had a voice of pure magic. He talked and talked and talked. Now he would fondle his giant lens; now he would grab a paper from his pocket and wave mathematical formulæ under my nose.

The lamplight glistened his glasses, shone on his bald skull, played in his whiskers, made a halo of the tobacco smoke weaving ropes about his head. Every time he drove home a puissant point he would snatch the pipe out of his beard and fire a bomb of smoke at my sweating face.

I listened, I say, and the sweat began to bubble down my cheeks. The little man's wizardly voice trapped my attention and held my eye on him and on his monstrous glass lens. Quite suddenly I became aware that Dr. Gulick Habighorst had something to say. You bet he did. And when he had finished my garments were damp on my limbs, my mouth was open, my feet slept under me, and my brain was whirling dizzily under the impact of those startling words.

As for the doctor, he sat trembling with excitement, his twig-like hands a-gesture painting queer, dancy shadows down the wall, his beard panting smoke at the clouded ceiling like a white bush taken fire.

"You understand? You understand? You understand?" The words trembled from his teeth. His hands flickered under my chin. "You see? You realize what all this may mean? You comprehend the marvel, the wonder of it, the terrible power of the thing? You comprehend? You understand?"

I understood, all right enough. If what my witchlike visitor had said proved true, there was going to be a thaumaturgy worked in Houglan Ra that *would* tremble the foundations of the universe; and I would be witness to the most amazing, the most astounding miracle of all this mad world. For the revelation amounted to this:

**DR. GULICK HABIGHORST** was a physicist and a lunarian—one who had devoted half a century to the study of the moon. For years he had examined the lunar phenomena in all its phases. India was the ideal locale for his scientific explorations. India, where the moon shone more vividly than elsewhere on the globe; where the lunar rays were less adulterated than in other zones. A decade ago, during observations made from certain localities—particularly the valley of Houglan Ra—he had come upon an astounding discovery.

This had to do with such vastly abstruse matters as electrolysis, atomic philosophy, analytic electrodynamics, and the advanced theories of Lwigon Blenderzog—a Viennese astronomer—on the doctrine of lunar atomizations. To a former stock broker and a present seeker of tiger hides, a little deaf from quinine and buzzing at the heels, these doctrines of advanced physics were as comprehensible as calculus to a wooden Indian. But, boiled down, they were fairly simple, if true:

All matter is composed of tiny electric particles known to science as atoms. An iron bar is composed of trillions of atoms. A man's thumb is composed of atoms. A box of candy, London Bridge, a pair of pants with lace trimming the bottom, a yellow canary and its wicker cage, a grand piano, a Krupp gun, a train of cars on the Rock Island Railroad, a mustache cup, the Woolworth Building and the stenographers peopling it and the garters on their legs and the gum in their mouths all composed of nothing but atoms. Now these atoms were held together by magnetism, and if this magnetism could be made negative the atoms would fly apart and their owners vanish in an instant. If the atoms in an iron bar were once released, the iron bar would vanish. Similarly the Woolworth Building and its contents would disappear in a flash, as would a box of candy or London Bridge.

And Dr. Gulick Habighorst had uncovered the method for releasing those atoms! A shaft of unadulterated moonlight thrown through a lens ground to certain proportions would do the trick. The lens had to be made capable of catching a particular type of moonbeam, the L-Ray. Dr. Gulick Habighorst had discovered the idiosyncrasies of this L-Ray, had encountered the unadulterated moonlight necessary to the experiments, and had perfected the necessary lens.

I finally got the words out of a mouth filled with dough. "You mean that a shaft of moonlight falling through that lens you have there on the table will destroy everything on which it falls? You mean, don't you, that you could focus a spot of moonlight passing through your lens on an object, and the object would fly into oblivion? Isn't that your idea? A sort of death ray from the moon?"

"That's it! That's it! That's it!" chanted the gnome. "I set the lens up on a tripod. The moonlight will pass through it and drop a shaft of light, the L-Ray, onto the sand. Any object whatsoever, on encountering that shaft of light, becomes nil. Just vanishes, that's all. It would destroy a human body in the wink of an eye, or a building, or a tree, or a whole forest. Train it on a city and sweep the city into naught. Train it on an army, and the army vanishes from the face of the earth. A terrible, terrific, unthinkable engine of destruction it can be—or a vast power for good. Engineers wish to tear down a bridge. They flash the L-Ray on the bridge, and it is gone.

"Curiously enough, the only objects my ray fails to destroy are glass and wet sand. Why, I have not yet ascertained. But the ray cannot penetrate and destroy glass; obviously it cannot, or the lens inducting it would be shattered in the process. Again, wet sand refuses demolition. Glass, after all, is composed of silicate sand, and there must be some power negative to the moonbeams in moist sand. Sand, then, and glass could be used as defenses against the ray. But you can imagine its ghastly potency for untold evil."

**HE MOPPED** his face, and I mopped mine.

"I've come to you," he went on, "because I need financial aid to perfect my lenses. I need at once twenty thousand pounds. Also I ask aid of you because there can be no scientific jealousy between us. You will back me as a business man."

"Doctor," I promised him, "if your lens is what you claim it to be, I will back you with the money. If you can prove to me—"

"Proof?" he squeaked. "I will I will give you proof—to-night! Now! You want to see the lens in action? Yes! To-night, then; the moon is splendid to-night. You know the river in the valley? There is a sandy bank not far from here where we shall set up the lens and experiment. You shall be shown, and satisfied. I have it! My pet canary shall contribute to the cause. That ought to be proof enough. And we can employ other objects to hand.

"We shall try bullets. Bullets cannot pass through the ray." He rubbed his palms together and chattered. "To-night you shall see for yourself. But you understand the awful peril your knowledge of this lens will place you under. There will be enemies who would sell their souls to—"

"*Sahib!*" Mardo's sudden voice made me jump as if kicked. Believe me, I had more than forgotten the Punjabi. I swung about on him, and the expression on his face gave my spine a tweak. His Adam's apple was moving up and down, and he was pointing his skinny thumb. "*Sahib,*" he said softly, "some one watches through the screen. They have been watching for some time. Look. The screen nearest the gun rack. *Ahee!*"

Dr. Gulick Habighorst flung about on his chair like a jumping-jack. Following the native's thumb, I let a chill shiver trickle down my back. Was I victim of imagination, or did I actually see a pair of porcine black eyes fastened like shoe buttons at a crack in the rattan blind? Half a split second they were there, boring the room and those of us in it with a level, unbending scrutiny. Then they were gone.

We dashed helter-skelter out of the bungalow. Dr. Habighorst got a long-barreled revolver out from under his whiskers; and I was mighty content to hold my Maynard in my fists. But if there had been any eyes at the screen, they had vanished into the darkness. Search as we would we could discover no trace of a possible prowler.

The fat moon hung yellow as gold in the sky above the cliffs. Down where the river sneaked the jungle murmured softly. Softly on the perfume-weighted breeze stole the sweet tinkle of the temple bell.

## CHAPTER III

# IN THE MOON-RAY

FEELING MYSELF A tinkling idiot, I carried the wicker cage housing the peeping yellow canary. Dr. Habighorst walked in the lead. He had insisted on shouldering the pack, despite my offers to carry it, and once more, among the green and black and purple shadows of the jungle bottom, he appeared to be a dodo. Mardo, toting the lantern, followed the aged scientist.

All I could see of the good doctor was his ridiculous pair of legs swinging through the wavering patches of lantern light, and the bulky black shadow of his pack.

We must have made a weird picture, the three of us—a strange processional creeping single file along that tortuous jungle path: a gnome bent double under a giant load; a skinny, stork-legged Hindu swinging a frustrated lantern; and a fat-head under a sun helmet, carrying in one fist a heavy rifle and in the other fist a highly incongruous canary cage.

The jungle was a tangle of banyans, cotton woods, creeper-woven palm thickets, and wedges of clumpy bamboo. Here or there a slant of moonbeams happened to stab through the jungle's roof; and every time we trod a pool of moonlight lying across our path Dr. Gulick Habighorst would mumble: "Aaah!"

I must admit my nerves were getting a bit wrenchy. Mardo got going on his "Ram-ram-ramming" again, and I told him if he didn't shut that jabber back into his Adam's apple I'd give him a ram on the beak. The Hindu himself was uneasy. About every two seconds he would jerk his head and peer into the shadows and mumble in his throat.

When I asked Mardo what the devil was wrong, he reminded me of the shoe-button eyes fastened at the crack in the bungalow screen. Also, he confided, Houglan Ra was inhabited at night by the souls of the Crimson Avengers of Jehan Ji.

The Crimson Avengers of Jehan Ji were legendary bandits who had once played evil all over the valley; jolly Brahmins who owned a penchant for roasting victims over slow fires and stringing old ladies up by the thumbs. Mardo's story didn't bother me much; for I was sure such gentlemen had never owned souls.

I was considerably more uneasy about the shoe buttons at the screen. Suppose somebody had been out there, listening, and had heard the doctor's story? And, then, the doctor's story! Suppose it really happened to make sense, and the doctor really happened to be a scientist and not a gnome or a nut! In that case I was certainly becoming a tool of fate. Good Lord, what if the lens was the real thing! Way back in my mind, you see, I was pretty certain the whole business was liver trouble and too much quinine, and a dream.

I told myself it was a dream as I walked along the trail; and then I twisted my ankle on a cottonwood root and was more than reassured of total reality.

The little doctor was pretty nervous, too. Before we had set out for the river he had frantically expressed the hope that our minds had gone the better of us and we had not seen eyes peeking through the screen. It would be nothing short of tragedy for us and for the unknowing world if another party had learned the secret. Suppose a Bolshevik emissary should get predatory hands on the lens; uncover the secrets of the L-Ray. The doctor trembled at the mention of such an idea. I trembled.

It would go hard with me if the world should learn of my knowledge in this affair. But there seemed little chance of such a disaster. Houglan Ra was out of the world; many, many miles out of the world.

**I CONFESS,** however, my breath came easier when we covered the three miles to the river, broke from a hedge of bamboos, and trudged down a sanded bank. Jungles at night are scarcely the jolliest roads to travel, especially when a member of one's party happens to carry in a sack on his shoulders a lens that could destroy at one focus the Woolworth Building. Dr. Habighorst scuttled across the sand; dumped his pack from his back; sought the sky with his queer glasses.

The moon had inched behind a film of smoky green cloud, and its sickly luminescence mantled the crooked river, glimmered dully on the surface of the muddy flood, and hung steamy shadows where the jungle flourished down to the water's edge.

Mardo squatted beside his lantern; never took eyes off the bamboos behind him. Gun across my knees, I crouched beside the Punjabi. Dr. Gulick Habighorst got busy with his sack. He looked for all the world like some subterranean wizard preparing an instrument for charms. Out of the sack came a tripod and a score of smaller astronomical instruments.

With elaborate care he screwed his giant lens into a drum fitted across the apex of the tripod. Erected, the tripod stood some ten feet above ground, so that the lens would shed a spot of light encompassed by the tripod legs, a spot of light that should be about eight feet in diameter.

Muttering in his whiskers, the little doctor scurried about on his spidery bowlegs; sighted the moon through an instrument not unlike a quadrant; then set the tripod in position on a fan of sand at the very lip of the river. After adjusting the lens to an angle where it would face the moon and admit the reflected moon-rays, he stooped to slap handfuls of river water over the sand beneath the tripod. When he had done he dragged his canvas sack away from the instrument; backed away from the tripod, and came to sit beside me on the sand.

You can see the three of us, then, squatting in a row on the bank of that green, slimy river. Across the river a ridge of ink-black crags jutted raggedly against the indigo sky. Behind us hung a wall of murmurous jungle, steamy, redolent of decaying vegetation, whispery in the fetid darkness. Screened by clouds, the moon cast a weak phantom-glow, throwing ghostly shadows across the wrinkled water that lapped sibilantly against the fan of sand where the tripod stood.

Wiggling his hands at the tripod some eight feet distant, the doctor talked. He spoke of the possibilities of his L-Ray lens. Imagine a fleet of war planes armed with projectors fitted with the lens. Such planes could wing on moonlight nights over a sleeping city, focus their ray-catching lenses on a town, and sweep the town into blankness.

Imagine one man armed with such a projector. By training the ray on an enemy he could dash his victim into swift oblivion, and the world could never know.

No wonder my brain whirled; no wonder I did not believe! No wonder I thought my companion a derelict madman, a pseudo-scientist, or a quinine-phantasy.

Still, he spoke rationally. And here we were, sitting on the bank of the river, glaring at the tripod, waiting for the moon to come clear and light the lens, and prove!

"While we await the passing of the clouds," I heard the doctor saying, "let us come to an understanding, Reven Staffard." He turned his goggles on me; stroked his beard with gentle fingers. "I have picked you to be my partner; have chosen you from a world of souls quite at random. It was the only way. But I must have some manner of security.

"First, you must swear you will not, until such time as I see fit, reveal a single item of the phenomena you are about to witness. You must vow never to speak a single word to a single soul. Your Hindu boy will not understand, and is therefore safe.

"Of course, you cannot rob from me my lens. You might desire so to do, when you see it in action. But in your unpracticed hands it would prove useless. You do not know the exact angle at which it must be set. You do not know at which moon-phase it could become potent. I have salved the glass with a chemical compound known only to me, without which the lens is impotent. Thus I am defended from theft of my secret.

"But to perfect my lenses I need money. Can you write me a check? Can you give me a sum of gold when you have seen this experiment? Could you arrange for me this added security? Listen. I will give you a demonstration to-night. You will be convinced. After this demonstration you will give me, say, ten thousand pounds—a check or gold. I will return to my laboratories in Calcutta. You will stay here. I return in a month's time. Meantime you have kept absolute silence. Then when I come back with my augmented apparatus we can journey farther into the hills, experiment further, and finally go to Berlin to disseminate our powers.

"Of that business development we can speak later. Just now I desire a gesture of security. I will demonstrate my lens. Will you award me the money and the promise of absolute silence?"

**"IF YOUR** lens will—er—make things like iron bars vanish," I admitted, "I will promptly give you a check for ten thousand pounds. I will give you a check for twenty thousand pounds. I will write you the check here and now. I will return to the bungalow and hand you cash to the amount of five hundred pounds as a starter."

If his lens would work, it was worth a million pounds. But I was chuckling in my throat. Of course the thing was a fake. No doubt it would fail in its demonstration, the doctor would frantically claim a misadjustment or something, pack up his bag and disappear. Might as well humor the queer little lunatic. Of course he had a bolt loose in that copper dome of his.

"Agreed," he chuckled. "Listen, my friend. While we await the coming of the moon, would it not be well to go to your bungalow and get me those bank notes? Then, after the demonstration, I could depart at once for Calcutta.

"With the notes and your check and your vow of secrecy!" He seemed suddenly possessed of an electric vigor. "I could pack up and leave at once. I would not even stay to sleep. I have awaited financial succor so long, so long. The money. We are joint partners, then."

He thrust out his hand. I clutched it. It was dry as a twig. Mardo tapped on my shoulder, hunched closer, and whispered in my ear:

"But, *sahib*, there is evil down the wind. Evil. We are in great danger, *sahib*. Do not join this man and his enterprise. Danger! The souls of the Crimson Avengers flee on the jungle's breath."

I hopped around and got a clutch on that skinny rascal's throat. This mad affair had finally yanked my nerves into shreds. I wanted to tell that bearded little nut to pack up and go to hell. I wanted to choke the nonsense out of Mardo. I was letting a maniac and a night in the jungle make an idiot out of me, too. A death ray from the moon. Bah! A native who felt things invisible with his fingertips. Bah! Too much quinine! Too much quinine!

"Shut up that blithering Crimson Avenger nonsense, Mardo!" I yelped into his brass-colored Hindu face. "Pick up your lantern. We're getting out of here. I'm a fool to have stayed so long. I'm going back to the bungalow and get some sleep. What a fairy tale I've fallen for!" I jerked around on the man who called himself Dr. Gulick Habighorst.

"I've had enough of this fool racket!" I snarled. "Yes, doctor, I have faith in your lens. Sure I have. Be a good little boy and come back to the bungalow with us and—"

"The moon!" shrieked the doctor. Like a marionette suddenly jerked by all its wires, he bounced to his feet, got a finger into the air, and pointed at the sky. "The moon! The moon! The moon!" His voice echoed and reechoed among the black crags across the river. "The moon! The moon! The moon!"

Sure enough, the moon. Those smoky green clouds had crawled away, and the moon sailed free against the vaulted dome of night, shedding its spectral rays down on the green river and the purple jungles and the ragged ridge of crags.

The silvery moonglow flung a shimmering shine across the water; made of the river a burbling, sneaking road of mercury. Far away a jackal howled, and the cliffs across the water howled too.

"The lens!" bawled the doctor's beard.

And the crags made phantom answer: "The lens!"

Truly enough, the lens. The moonlight shafted through the glass and cast a violet-hued spot of light on the fan of sand. The doctor's splayed bare feet were dancing intricate steps under his bulbous belly; his hands were dodging like excited little bats under my nose. Suddenly they dived under his beard, and came out clutching a fountain pen and a check book.

"Write me a check!" he shrilled. "Write me a check, make your vow of a month's silence, and I'll prove, I'll demonstrate, I'll prove!"

I KNEW at the time it was all too queer to be real; but I got the check book into my fumbly fingers and somehow or other managed to scrawl my signature under a note for fifty thousand pounds. By thunder, if his lens didn't work, I'd snatch that check out of his hands and stand on no gentle ceremony about his glasses, but smash him a whack on the nose!

He rammed the check into his pocket; yelped at me to lift a hand heavenward and swear to keep the secret of the night's proceedings. I lifted a fist at the sky, and swore out loud to never reveal the goings-on of that mad evening. Under my breath I added a few extra oaths for good measure.

I could hear Mardo swearing behind me. The skinny Hindu

had dodged away from the lens and the tripod as if they had been anathema. He stood backed to a hedge of banyans, and his scarecrow carcass was quivering like the bones of a skeleton in a gibbet I could hear the click of his chattering teeth, and I could hear the "ram-rams" stammering out of his jellied throat.

But I wasn't paying Mardo much attention, you can bet on that. I was glaring at Dr. Gulick Habighorst of the glassy, dollar-round eye, and the Niagara-like beard and spidery leg. I was glaring at the little scientist and glaring at his lens and the moon-ray cast by that lens. And the sweat leaked in rivers down my face, the feeling abandoned the palms of my hands, and the knees turned to water under me.

What do you suppose had happened? Dr. Gulick Habighorst had dodged up close to the tripod; turned on me a smile of triumph. And before my popping eyes he had flung his fountain pen at the moonbeams flooding in a tinted cone out of the lens. I say he flung the fountain pen. Yes, he did. I saw it in his fingers as he threw. He stood close to the lens and tripod, but he was mighty careful not to let his hand dodge into that shaft of inducted light. The pen flashed out of his fingers into the lens-shed rays—and disappeared.

Fountain pens—and this is not an advertisement—have, no doubt, put over some great ideas in their days. Fountain pens have signed well-meaning peace treaties, death warrants, billions of checks. But no fountain pen ever put over such a monstrous, momentous idea as was put over by that fountain pen which had vanished from the fingers of Dr. Gulick Habighorst, wielded in that lost, India-tainted valley of Houglan Ra.

I had just signed a check with that fountain pen, and it was just such a pen as inks the fingers of schoolboys every day. It had vanished under the rays of a lens set on a tripod on a fan of sand lapped by a jungle river. Vanished into nothingness—disappeared before a second could tick!

Right then I saw in my addled mind a livid picture. Buildings whisked into oblivion; men blotted out while they strolled a street; armies swept away into moonbeams. Blown, as Dr. Gulick Habighorst put it, into atoms. Reduced to electrons. Flicked into whiffs of ether.

**I GLARED** at Dr. Habighorst, at the tripod and the pool of moonlight cast by the lens on the sand, at the bony fingers which had held and thrown the fountain pen, at the moon bowling down the indigo sky overhead. A chuckle eeked from the doctor's whiskers, and he patted one of the tripod legs with an affectionate hand.

Moving sick feet, I edged toward the improbable instrument. The bewhiskered scientist turned his spectacles on me; stared owlishly; clucked like a hen.

"You begin to believe? You see those violet-tinted beams falling from my lens? You understand them, now; realize their unnatural power? Yes! They can whirl anything into nothingness—anything. Anything, as I previously explained, save glass and wet sand. Suppose you were to fall under that lens, into that shaft of light. You would vanish, Reven Staffard, like candle-flame brushed by a tornado. Suppose I were to walk into that cone of beams. There would be nothing left of me. Nothing except," he chuckled, "my glasses, of course."

He brushed a sleeve across his skull. With all the respect in the world I eyed his instrument. As yet I could not grapple with the tremendous import of the thing. What a shock such an instrument was going to deal the world. What power those who exploited it were going to own. Dizzy speculations throbbed through my mind.

"Look again," my companion murmured.

Brushing aside his beard, he fumbled fingers over his chest and tore a brass button from his linen jacket. For a moment he studied the brass button, holding it in the tips of his fingers.

"Watch closely," he advised.

I watched. He cautiously stretched his hand toward the ray that fell between the tripod's legs. A snap of the fingers.

The brass button was gone!

"There are nine brass buttons left on my jacket," he lectured impressively. "They would all vanish under the L-Ray thrown by my lens. Nine skyscrapers in the heart of New York could be vanished as readily. Buttons and buildings are composed of atoms. My ray disintegrates those atoms. Buttons and buildings disappear under the ray. So do you and I. Let us try again."

His words and his fingers quaked with excitement. Once again he dived a hand under his beard; yanked from his jacket his long-barreled revolver. "Look you, my friend. Bullets cannot pass through the ray. But let us try. Watch."

Gun in fist, he swung around and aimed at an object floating down the moon-illumined breast of the stream. It looked like a log, but it wasn't a log. I caught the gleam of ghoulish eyes set in knobs poked above water, and a long, knobby snout. The gun in the doctor's withered hand jerked, exploded, and spat flame. The echoes of the shot caromed down the crags, and a spout of water spurted where the bullet struck close to the crocodile's snout.

The doctor handed the revolver to me. "Get behind the tripod," he instructed. "Have the ray fall between your gun muzzle and your mark out there in the river. See if you can drive a bullet between the legs of the tripod. Try a shot."

I placed myself in such a position that it would be necessary for the fired bullet to whiz through the light falling from the lens. I fired. No bullet went farther than that cone of violet light. No spout of water jumped on the breast of the stream I handed the revolver back to its owner, grabbed off my sun helmet and fanned a sweating face.

Through buzzing ears I heard the old man offer to try again. Once more he shot a bullet at the sand and dug a smoking hole near his toe. Again he aimed at the spot of light under the tripod and fired. No bullet disturbed the wet sand flooded by the circle of light. There was no hole. And it didn't dry my face for me, either.

"**ALL** right, Reven Staffard?" the doctor was asking softly.

"Are you convinced? You saw what happened to the fountain pen, to the brass button, to the bullets. Good. But let us try a living object. Let us see if my ray from my lens can destroy the animate, can blow to atoms and make to vanish a body of life. My canary. Let us, as a final test, try my canary. It lives, it breathes, moves. You can hear it sing."

The bird was singing as he spoke. Petrified, I stood gaping at the tripod while the doctor ducked away and came back with the wicker cage in his hand. I didn't want to see that tiny object of life flickered out by a mere spot of lens-thrown moonbeams. But I couldn't take my eyes from the thing. My throat was knotting in my neck and the pulse drumming in my temples as my wizard of a companion stretched the bird cage toward the tripod. The canary dodged and skipped and trilled in its tiny prison. For a moment the old man studied the moon, watched the canary, turned his owlish, glassy gaze on me.

My feet were lead, and a thunderclap wouldn't have taken my fascinated gaze from the cage in those twig-like hands.

Suddenly the old man squawked. "Now!" His hand whipped out. Canary and cage must have sailed right under my sweat-leaking nose. Canary and cage were gone!

The voice from the white beard was solemn as a funeral knell. "Vanished under the L-Ray. Cage. Canary. Gone. Blown to atoms, to oblivion. And now that you know, now that you are sworn to secrecy, now that you have given me the money and I can return to cash your check in Calcutta and buy instruments, chemicals, apparatus to—"

I think we both must have heard the sound at the same instant. I don't quite know how it was. At any rate, we whirled about like a pair of dancers timed to music on a stage. That sound! That queer, gurgling, giggling sound!

We jumped around on our heels, forgot the tripod and the lens and the L-Ray. My sun helmet dropped from my nerveless fingers and rolled at my boots. A rattly, crackly cry shook from the doctor's snowy beard, and his face went the color of banana meat.

It was Mardo. We had forgotten the native. We remembered him now. He had been standing, his back to the hedge of banyans. Now he was sitting, back to the hedge of banyans. His arms hung limp at his sides. His legs were spread apart and his toes pointing stiffly at the sky. He had thrown back his head to look at the moon, but he wasn't looking at the moon.

The moon was looking at Mardo. It was painting his face the most nauseous yellow tinge conceivable. And it was making to gleam the rivers of red enamel that welled from the Adam's apple of Mardo's gaunt throat. Never again would Mardo mumble a prayer to Rama, seventh incarnation of Vishnu, out of that Adam's apple. A knife had cut it to the core.

CHAPTER IV

# MAD COMBAT

**MAYBE THE SOULS** of the Crimson Avengers of Jehan Ji had done it. Right then, in the valley of Houglan Ra, I could have believed any fairy story. But I remembered the eyes that had been at the screen at the bungalow; and believe me, it was easy to imagine a very human hand creeping out of those banyans to draw a knife across an unwary Hindu's throat.

Mardo's finger tips had failed him at the time of need. I knew why. He had been watching a gnome make objects vanish under a tripod. Better finger tips than Mardo's would have failed under such circumstances.

Dr. Gulick Habighorst had turned into a cartoon made of stone, and Heaven only knows the occult power that pleased to loan vitality to my own poor feet. But I hopped over to my Maynard rifle in no short order. I wanted to feel that gun in my fist, and I wanted it badly. Mardo looked like the very devil spraddled against those banyans with blood pumping out of his neck and rippling down over his ribs.

The doctor got a whistly screech out of his beard.

"His throat's cut! His throat's cut! Somebody cut his throat!" The ragged crags across the river screeched in turn. "His throat's cut! His threat's cut! Somebody cut his throat! Cut his throat!"

I'm not a brave man, and never was. I can't talk smartly back to New York cops with faces like Hamburg steaks. Once, at Contalmaison, I got an idea a Boche raiding party was coming over to cut up my telephone station, and I ran so fast I almost caught up with the colonel. But courage is a flighty emotion; goes hand in hand with rage. And I was mad as a hatter about that Punjabi. His prayers and predilections might have prickled my neck at times, but he had been half around the Orient with me, and his curry and rice and loyalty had been the best in the world.

Sobbing with fury, I dashed into the banyans, intent on riddling with bullets the first human in sight. There weren't any humans in sight among the banyans, though. It was black as a witch's curse in there. I yelled, and kicked among mats of vines and roots, scratched my face to ribbons, tore my legs in brambles, whipped at every shadow with the barrel of my gun.

My uproar started a legion of bats into flight, small animals whisked under foot, and a heron or something went hooting past my head like an evil thought.

In half a minute I was floundering in a pool of cobalt darkness, struggling with nobody but myself. After I had walked into a spider web and hung a thick veil across my face I was not too sure about the Crimson Avengers after all. There couldn't have been any other human beings in that jungle of Houglan Ra. Human beings wouldn't have—

Then I heard a scream. A human scream, if a scream from Dr. Gulick Habighorst could have been termed human.

The dolorous wail coiled through the banyans, coming from

the beach by the river. "Help! Help, Reven Staffard, save me! Sa-a-a-ve me-e-e!"

Thrashing like a maniac, I fought back to the river bank; plunged from the banyans almost at the spot where what was left of Mardo sat in a puddle of blood.

There was the doctor, jigging and dodging on one side of the tripod. His revolver was in his fist, and he was yelping like a terrified poodle and moving as St. Vitus never had moved. And dodging and jigging—it was like a game of tag, I swear—on the other side of the tripod was a squatty-built nan clad in a white cotton suit. In one hairy fist he waved an automatic; in the other fist a drippy knife. His eyes were shoe buttons glowing from the shadow of his sun helmet brim. His purple face was as German as the war-time mustache of Kaiser Wilhelm.

**"SO!" HE WAS** bellowing. "You haf a German name, und you plan to sell this instrument of death to dot Yankee! *Himmel!* Traitor? It is to me you sell dot lens. Berhaps I kill you und take it myself. I heard you. Und I saw dot lens vork, yess! Und I take it back with me to Germany. Fur Deutschland! *Ach, Gott!* Me und Schmitty, ve grab it. *Ja!*"

"I never saw you before!" the doctor bawled. "Get away from here! You can have the lens. To hell with the lens. Don't touch me with that knife. Help! I'm going to be murdered. Save me! Save me!" His voice attained an astonishing falsetto. "Save me! Staffard!"

Flinging rifle to shoulder, I stepped over Mardo's red legs and pumped a bullet at the German's purple countenance. Whether I missed aim or the bullet was dissolved by the rays from the tripod lens, I don't know. Dr. Habighorst's assailant was playing a furious ring-around-the-rosy, trying to catch the doctor, trying to keep away from the spot of light under the tripod.

At the sound of my gun he went up in the air like a jack-rabbit and let a livid squall out of his lungs.

"Your bullets von't go through the ray," he yelled, scrambling to keep the tripod between his bulk and my gun. Dodging suddenly, he let go a shot from the automatic that knocked a chip out of my ear. I tried to get a bead on him as he did so. The next instant a heavy missile clubbed against my spine and flung me sprawling; knocked the rifle from my hands. I got to my feet in time to get a flat stone in the face, and the next moment I was grappling with another white cotton suit and German face.

This second German had popped out of the brambles behind me. The shock of his rush sent us rolling in frenzied embrace; knocked the wind out of me. I should have noted the first German's mention of Schmitty. I had been so astonished at finding one German in the valley of Houglan Ra I had not noticed anything. However, I was now giving No. 2 my full attention.

He got a scissors hold on me, and I thumped manfully at his face. Then he worked a half Nelson while I busily kicked his shins. Clutched together, we rolled down the sand to the water's edge and back again, floundered into a mess of brambles and out again, pounded and whacked and gouged and tore and scratched. Once Mardo got mixed up in the wrestling match. That wasn't nice—it wasn't nice at all. We got rid of Mardo, gained our feet, toppled back to the sand.

After a brief scrabble I found myself on top. My enemy had my hands pinned under me, my ankles twisted with his, and my face pressed into his yellow mop of hair.

I had his face rammed hard into the sand, and had only to await his speedy suffocation. Neither of us chose to move, and there we sprawled. This gave me a chance to see the gnomelike scientist and German No. 1 grappling in a little wrestle of their own. It didn't take me long to see what they were trying to do. Each was battling to shove the other under the tripod! Both were fighting like fury; and the German was busily trying to thrust his knife into the doctor's abdomen while the doctor strove to prevent it.

Back and forth and around the tripod they fought. Now they were knee-deep in the river, churning the water to lather; now they were struggling across the sand, cursing, gasping, panting oaths. The German had a black fist in the doctor's snowy whiskers. The doctor had a thumb in the German's left eye. Every once in a while they would rock against the tripod; dance away squealing.

**DURING** that titanic encounter a queer thing happened. Desperate as was my own situation, I noticed it. A thin silver cigarette case fell from the doctor's coat; was kicked under their tramping feet. I swear, that little fighting dwarf went crazy. With insane strength he battled out of the German's grasp, stooped, snatched up that cigarette case, popped it into his jacket.

What was the fool doing? My Maynard, an automatic, and his own revolver lay within reach on the sand; and he had grabbed up that trifling trinket.

I bawled at him; told him to get hold of a gun. Too late. The German was on top of him like a wild cat. His spidery legs crumpled under him and he fell with a shriek. What's more, he came within half a foot of going into the pool of moonlight under the tripod. It brought six curses out of my teeth when I thought of what would happen should either of those battling maniacs roll into the shaft of light dropped by the lens.

Well, the little old man wasn't going to last long under the German's pounding fists. Blood leaked into the white whiskers, burbling from his mouth. His flailing hands had become scarlet twigs. His big bare feet looked like puddings, smashed by the German's stamping boots. The crags across the sneaky river echoed with his soprano screams.

But he was putting up an astonishing battle. He kept fighting the German away from the tripod. He clawed that Teutonic countenance into a bloody ham. He fought like a jaguar, and the German fought like a gorilla. The moonlight gleamed on their writhing bodies.

Mardo's corpse, recumbent near the banyans, looked on. A gavial jabbed its knobby eyes out of the river near shore, and looked on. Pinned to the ground atop my enemy, I looked on. They were fighting, those men. Fighting for the possession of a power that would shake the foundations of the world.

Suddenly I found my lungs strong with breath; knew it was time to aid the doctor. With a savage wrench I loosed my enemy's hold on my hands. We rolled over. He kicked a terrible hold, his legs on mine. I went down, bent into a knot, twisted into a painful contortion. His hands trapped my throat. My hands fastened on his neck. Face pressed to face, legs tangling, bodies locked, we staggered and went lurching across the sand in a macabre dance.

Whirling faster and faster, we went crashing into the banyans, floundering off in the darkness, battling among the trees, away from the bank of the river. He didn't loosen his choking grip, nor did I loosen mine. I couldn't see. The tongue swelled in my mouth. The roof of my head burst into flames. My arms, legs, feet died. We went down together. Vines lashed our feet; darkness closed in.

**IMPOSSIBLE** to tell how long I lay there in the darkness, fighting for the breath that would bring me life, holding in an iron clutch a corpse. For the German had become a corpse. His lungs had given out first, and his fingers had unhooked their strangling hold.

I knew he was dead, for his body had turned to sponge. I didn't want to lie there beside him, but for a long time I couldn't get up. Wet vines brushed my face. The smell of moldy jungle earth and mud and blood and sweat plugged my nostrils. I could catch a faint odor of orchid, too.

That dreadful creature sprawled beside me had, on recent occasion, been chewing cloves. I remember wondering where he had obtained the cloves. I remember wondering, too, where those two Germans had come from. Memory yanked me out of a coma, and abruptly I heard the screams.

They came from the direction of the river. Long, drawn-out screams, and shrill. Like the banshee whoops of ambulance sirens pulsing into midnight. Screams that froze the blood in my veins and made me fight to move my legs. I couldn't move those legs—not for a long time. I had come within an ace of being choked to death, and my legs just wouldn't forget it. It wasn't jolly to lie there on the floor of that Houglan Ra jungle beside a spongy German corpse smelling of cloves while those awful wails twisted out of the dark. It was the rottenest sensation in the world.

How I tried to get to my feet! When I finally did manage to stand on legs of warm rubber the screaming had ceased to be. There were echoes. Echoes tossed by ragged black crags. Echoes out of a past. Whether that past was ten minutes, ten years, or ten hours I have never been able to determine.

Somehow—it took years—I fought my way out of the banyan jungle, and after a dizzy eternity knew I was standing on the bank of the river. Yes, I was on the sandy river shore. There was the river, murmuring off through the flower-scented gloom. There were the crags across the mercury-colored flood. Crags whence voices, shadowy, tiny voices, lingered to wail. Black, raggedy crags stabbing at an indigo sky.

The moon lurked low in that indigo sky, I noticed. Soon it would be gone. But it was bright enough for me. It illumined the face of my dead Punjabi lying like an emptied scarecrow at the edge of the thicket. It scattered its ethereal rays down the river bank and picked out such objects as the doctor's emptied sack, my Maynard rifle, the doctor's long-barreled revolver, a German automatic strewn across the sand.

I noticed, besides, the lantern Mardo had carried, still upright and flickering bravely where first it had been set down. And I wanted to notice something else, but I didn't. I stared, wildly sought the shadows bounding the jungle's rim. I hunted the thickets with my eye. At long last I began to shout.

"Doctor!" I caterwauled. "Dr. Gulick Habighorst! Oh, doctor, where are you?" And the crags across the river wailed: "Oh, doctor! Where are you? Are you? You?"

That was the only answer. No—there was one other. I glared. I glared and my heart became a turnip and the blood in my veins turned to milk. I saw the answer. There were footprints spattered all over the fan of sand where the tripod stood. The footprints of fighting men. But there were not any footprints under that tripod standing close to the water's edge. The spot of moon-ray shed through the lens onto the sand didn't show a single footprint. It simply made a violet-tinted circle on the sand.

The sand had been disturbed; there was a mark there. There I saw an imprint that could only have been made by two bodies, locked in fighting embrace, and fallen between the legs of the tripod.

Those bodies might have rolled on into the river, but I knew they had not. Bodies would vanish to nothingness under that tripod where the violet spot of moonlight lay.

The spot of light cast by the lens on the sand showed the mark where those bodies had flopped. The bodies had gone. Only one object remained. I crept up closer, panting, like a boy sneaking up on a snake. I stared, and the object stared back at me. Stared owlishly, reflecting the moonlight. I wanted to die, I can tell you. I glared at those glistening eyes, and wanted to die.

The story was told. There in the center of that lens-shed spot of light lay—the doctor's glasses.

"Two objects resist the ray," I remember whispering to myself. "Two objects refuse demolition under the lens—wet sand, and glass."

Then the Maynard was in my hand, and the moon had gone. I raised my rifle and pulled the trigger. Once—twice. Again,. The third shot went home, and the great glass lens exploded in a shower of winging slivers. Clutching the rifle to my chest, I galloped into the banyans and started a race for the bungalow.

CHAPTER V

# THE MOON SETS

**NO, I DID** not bag my tiger and obtain prize gavial skins up there in the valley of Houglan Ra. The fact is, I didn't stay. I didn't wait for the arrival of my friend Bradshaw. The truth is, I hiked out of Houglan Ra, and I must have made a pretty wild hike, because I ended up in a mission hospital in Pangalore. Was I in the mission hospital a week, or was it six? I've quite forgotten. But I must have had it seriously. The head of the institution told me I came wandering into town as mad as a March hare.

He called me into his office and told me about it on the day I was discharged and to leave for Bombay. He told me I had raved like a fool about a gnome and a dodo. He told me I had chattered for hours on end—delirium of the worst kind—about a certain lens that would capture an L-Ray and obliterate a building or a canary in a cage. He told me I had raved about Hindus with cut throats, about unknown Germans who chewed cloves, and about men who had been blown to atoms.

Do you know what he said to me?

"Staffard," he said, "it's a wonder you're alive. You've been insane for days. You came marching into Pangalore one morning, ragged and crazy as a starved *fakir*. Know what I think? I'm wondering if you hadn't been wandering about those Houglan Ra jungles late at night. It looked to me as if you'd gotten a bit moonstruck."

**HOLMES BRADSHAW**, the gaunt Kelantan naturalist, let out a monster oath when he caught sight of me at the other end of the hotel veranda. He came wading through the crowd like a mad mother in a jammed kindergarten, and he stepped on a fat coffee planter's bad corn and didn't turn around to apologize.

"Staffard!" he yelped. "Reven Staffard, no less!" He was cracking the knuckles of my hand. "I say, you damned idiot, where the devil you been? How come you're back here in Bombay? And what in the name of the Seven Flat Cats of Assasta happened up there at my place in Houglan Ra? I couldn't find a house boy on the premises. The bungalow was run to rot—doors left open, guns stolen, specimens wandered off. And, say, listen!" His hand crushed mine. He made a hoarse, hot whisper of his voice.

"There'd been hell to pay up there. Murder, no less. By Heaven, I found some weird things up there. A fresh vulture-picked skeleton down on a beach by the river! And some other things I've got to show you. What the devil went on? I shot the biggest tiger I've ever seen back in the jungle, and down on the river I knocked off the world's biggest crocodile. You've got to come up to my room where we can talk. I've got to talk to you, Staffard! Up to my room! Right away!"

Once in his room he dashed around like an excited boy. I sat in a chair near a window. I was sick to my heels, I can tell you that. He had some things he wanted to show me, and he showed them.

And everything he exhibited made me sicker. He dug those awful exhibits out of a box from under his bed. A tripod. A canvas sack containing a scatter of queer, astronomical instruments. A German automatic, orange with rust. A long-barreled revolver, tarnished to the color of grass. My cheeks must have also tarnished to the color of grass as Bradshaw placed those exhibits, one by one, in a row on the floor at my feet. But the naturalist didn't notice.

"Look at that stuff," he panted. "If that isn't the damnedest! I picked up that truck down on the beach along the river. Scattered all around. There was a human skeleton lying there, I tell you, and all this truck strewn over the sand. Tripod standing near the water's edge.

"It's got my brain stopped, I tell you. This revolver, for example." He picked up the doctor's revolver; broke open the cartridge chamber. "Here's a mystery for you, by Heaven. Look at the shells in this thing. Every other one was a blank cartridge. What the hell?"

Yes, what the hell? Every other shell a blank cartridge! What the hell, indeed! Do you remember? First the doctor fired the gun; his bullet struck. Then I fired the gun; my bullet never did! Every other shell in that tarnished long-barreled revolver was a blank! I stared at that revolver, and my brain turned a flip-flop under my hair. Bradshaw was talking again:

"Now, listen," he was demanding, "This whole thing is queer, terrible. Something awful must have taken place down on the beach. First of all, what became of the two German chaps I sent up there to go shooting with you? Did you see them at all?" The naturalist's voice was shaky. "I'm wondering if you ever saw 'em? I say, Staffard, we've got to clear this up! They were friends of mine—Brokmann and Schmitt. Collectors. I met 'em in Allahabad, and sent 'em up to stay with you until I came.

"Both good fellows. Old German war veterans. Never got over the war. A bit cracked on this fatherland stuff. Brokmann had been on Hindenburg's staff. But fine chaps, just the same. I sent 'em up there to stay with you, and now—"

For a long, long minute Bradshaw couldn't speak. "I reckon they're dead. Couldn't find a trace of Schmitt. But that automatic on the beach was Brokmann's. I've come to the conclusion that skeleton must have been Schmitt. And look—"

OUT FROM under the bed he dragged a crocodile skin. Hardly necessary for me to state my brain was so paralyzed by that time I didn't have the gray matter to wonder what that crocodile hide had to do with it. Bradshaw held up the smoke-colored hide. His voice came out of a deep and distant well.

"See this gavial skin? Twenty-two feet long! I was picking

up that stuff on the sand when this monster floated by on the surface of the river. Couldn't resist. Got him with one shot. That stuff on the beach wasn't the half of it! Look at this!"

He was almost shouting. I could hardly hear him. I was staring through a lemon-colored mist. He had dropped the gavial skin; yanked a tin box out of his jacket, and dumped a little heap of junk into his palms. Junk, he called it. Junk? It wasn't junk to me! It hung the eyes almost out of my head. He handed the pieces to me, one by one; and I clutched them in fingers made of brittle ice.

"It's the damnedest litter of junk I've ever seen," he said. "A fountain pen; ten brass buttons; a belt buckle; a German war cross. That Iron Cross belonged to Brokmann, by Heaven! And this cigarette case. And this queer little folding box of sticks. By golly, Staffard, the whole thing has got me stumped forty ways! Just look at that junk! And wait till you see what that folding box of sticks does. Wait till you hear where that stuff came from. Where do you think, Staffard?

"I found that junk in the stomach of that crocodile I shot. That junk was in the gavial's stomach. In the gavial's stomach! Think of it, man—in that monster gavial's stomach! Think of it!"

I thought of it. I thought of that monster gavial's stomach. Lord knows why my heart didn't stop. I guess it did, for a few minutes. In those icicle fingers of mine I slowly turned the objects that had come out of that huge crocodile's stomach. A fountain pen. Ten brass buttons—*ten* of them! A belt buckle. A German war cross that had belonged to Brokmann. A silver cigarette case. And a little folding box of sticks that could do something queer.

I glared at that folding box of sticks. My fingers must have pressed a lever, for the folding box of sticks *did* do something queer. The rest of the junk went clattering from my hands; and I found myself holding a little wicker canary cage. A tiny object no bigger than a pearl dropped from those magical wicker sticks. I didn't say it was a pearl—I said it was no bigger than a pearl. It was the skull of a canary!

**BRADSHAW'S** voice—the echo of a ghost's echo—was saying: "Only the devil knows what these things can mean. What was that tripod? What could have been going on down there on the sandy beach? There must have been a third party. Say this third party had been fighting with Schmitt and Brokmann. That's the way it looked. He killed Schmitt, and that was Schmitt's skeleton." It was not. It was Mardo's skeleton. "Anyway, he had fought Brokmann. While they fought together they rolled under the tripod thing.

"There was a pair of glasses lying under the tripod, by the way. Must have been knocked from this third party's nose. At any rate, they rolled under the tripod and right out into the river. And it just happened so this giant gavial I shot swam along and grabbed 'em both while they were under the river."

He mopped his face, which looked like a wet pear. "That junk from the gavial's stomach was in their pockets," he whispered on. "The belt buckle and Iron Cross Brokmann always wore. Whose that other stuff was, God only knows. That fountain pen, those buttons, that trick cage, that cigarette case."

Indeed, God alone knew to whom those articles belonged; and He chose to reveal. Somehow or other I had dropped the magic cage to pick up the thin silver cigarette case. It was the one the doctor had dropped and snatched back to his bosom. Perhaps my thumb nail snapped it open. At any rate, it opened.

It did not contain cigarettes. Apparently its owner had used it as a safety-deposit vault for valuable papers. An aged, yellow newspaper clipping fell to the floor. My sick fingers unfolded the clipping, and my sick eyes read the following item:

> Daniel Perry, former vaudeville entertainer, wanted for extraordinary astronomy swindle. Obtains money from wealthy Back Bay science devotee by exceedingly involved scheme exposed by Harvard physicist. Posing as a—

There was a photograph of Daniel Perry heading the column. That was all I wanted of that! Another strip of paper, unwadded, proved to be my check for fifty thousand pounds. The check with which that lunarian was going to depart for Calcutta while I kept silent for a month. The third sheet of paper, unfolded, disclosed a faded lithographing. A handbill. The photograph at the top of the handbill was identical with that on the newspaper clipping. Bald head, beard, owlish glasses and all. The picture of Dr. Gulick Habighorst.

Writ large beneath it was the legend: "All This Week. Professor Daniel Perry Habighorst. Master Mystifier. King of Conjuring. World's Greatest Magician."

## "MOON UP"

Theodore Roscoe has a few words to say about his story "Moon Up," which appears in this issue—and which we think certainly establishes him as a story-teller of the first rank. Mr. Roscoe:

Perhaps you *Argosy* readers would be interested in a note concerning "Moon Up." Also I'd like to grab the bull by the golden horns and say a word in my own defense before some friend boomerangs certain parts of the story at my person.

In the first place there isn't any valley of Houglan Ra. Granted. But there are a lot of spots like it scattered about the Orient. A good share of the atmosphere was handed me by my mother, who was born in North India and spoke Hindee before she could speak English. The Mardo of the yarn was a house boy of hers; and an uncanny old rascal he was. He used to pull off a lot of hoorah about his finger tips and some of it wasn't so hoorah. My mother lived in India some score of years and this Mardo served her a decade, and the fellow was a pretty weird boy. Could read omens and guess fortunes with an accuracy to make one uncomfortable. (I might add that his finger tips were uncannily adept at closing over articles of value and he left the family's service under suspicion.)

Now a little native girl in a neighboring town near the family's mountain home managed to disappear. The villagers and my grandfather hunted high and low, concluding she had been lunched upon by a vagrant tiger. And (with apologies to Ripley's "Believe It Or Not") they found her remains—earrings, toe rings, beads and some other aids to indigestion in *exactly the same locale* as were found the explanations to my story. If you don't believe it I can't exhibit the objects as the naturalist in my story did, but I'll meet you in front of the Brasserie Terminus in Algiers next fall and fight for the family's honor. Because it's true!

So there aren't any gavials twenty-two feet long, eh? Well, there was a gavial skeleton in the Jardin des Plantes in Paris measuring twenty-one feet seven inches, and any naturalist can tell you how long he'd be with his coat on. Too long to toy with.

And as for the moon, I can only apologize for it as Reven Staffard did in his story. Go out into your backyard and study it some fine night. I've watched it a good many times rise in the African sky; and east of Suez they say it's even brighter. But take a good look at it above your own elm tree in your own yard. It's like a woman. Mysterious. You can never see the other side. No reason for it being there and yet you want it there. And it's the darnedest thing you've ever seen. Just the agent to make a good man disappear. *'Alikum salaam!*

THEODORE ROSCOE.

# THE BLUE CAT OF BUDDHA

*Deep in the jungles of Siam was the treasure that
had inspired a thousand Oriental legends; but
Johnny Ash and his friend found the legends paled by
the reality of the amazing guardian of the treasure*

# PROLOGUE

**HOLMES BRADSHAW TOLD** me this story in Saigon, and I put it on paper as one of the strangest tales to ever come from that land where all stories are strange.

We were sitting out the evening on the Hôtel Napoléon III veranda, facing Rue Catinat; cozy in a corner away from the chatter of French colonials trying to play the social game in that Oriental hole. Suddenly, under shadow of his enormous pith helmet, Bradshaw's face went queer. His hand, in the act of conveying a virgin (vermouth and gin) to his lips, hung poised in mid-air.

"Listen!" he demanded.

I listened. Indoors, an orchestra had started to play for the dance. The pulsing skip-beat of an American fox trot throbbed out into the dusk. Bradshaw beat time with a toe, then asked: "You know that song?"

"Do I?" I rasped. "It's one of the things I came out East to escape. Jazz music. That bit of rot in particular. For the last two years that's all you could hear in the States—that song. Every stage on Broadway has shouted it. Night after night on the radio. The phonograph next door and the piano across the street. You don't know how they ride a thing like that in America. Two years. At first I rather liked the thing. Silly, but a bit different. Now I'd like to choke the bird who wrote it. He made a cold million off it, you know. It's *the* hit. They played it all the way over on the boat. Now I see it's got Saigon by the ear. Do I know it!"

The gaunt Kelantan naturalist chuckled, and drank. The jazz band swung into the nervous chorus, a saxophone convulsing the melody. Every loud speaker in America would be spouting the same thing that evening.

That song! Those six weird starting notes that swung into rhythmic ragtime so different from the usual you had to remember it. First you liked it. Then you hated it. But you couldn't escape the thing.

"Can't get away from it even in Asia," I snarled. "Bah!"

Bradshaw laughed. "You think you know that song, do you? Well, I know it, too. Two years ago I was in New York City. Went to see a big theater that was just opening. That little song was breaking on Broadway, and the theater featured the thing. The guy who wrote it sang it on the stage. I could have died in my seat when I heard that music. You think you know the song? Well, you don't know the first thing about it. It puts me in mind of a story, old man, that's the wildest story ever told. It puts me in mind of the maddest piece of adventure I ever knew. Draw up a chair and I'll tell you the yarn. Listen."

This is the story he told me:

## CHAPTER I

# IN THE GULF OF SIAM

**TWENTY HOURS UP** the Gulf of Siam, the good ship Houri exploded a cargo of contraband hidden in her hold, and went off like a cannon cracker. I was standing at the rail when the blow came, and the jar knocked me off my feet. I slammed my face against a stanchion and went over the rail, unconscious as a log. And I'd have drowned if the red-head hadn't been right there on the spot and saved my life.

Some mighty queer bits of humanity comb the beach down the China coast, but that red-head took the prize. I saw him first in Penang. I saw him again at Singapore; and later up at Hue. It's a bad road to travel if you don't go first-class; and most of them go down. The fever and alcohol get them first, then they take to opium for the finish. But (and he wasn't traveling first cabin, by any means) that red-head seemed to hang on.

He was singing for his meals in Penang, and his voice was a dead giveaway. You know the type that sings at the sheet music counter in the five-and-ten? That red-headed Yankee was just the essence of that type. Thin and jiggly and nervous; clad in a tight-fitting pin-stripe suit pinched at the waist, a green shirt, a purple tie, miserable patent leather shoes. Fingers, yellow from nicotine-stain, snapping to keep dexterous time. A freckled, blue-eyed face under a weedy mop of hair the color of carrots. And a voice that came out through his nose, and made you think of Times Square, Forty-second Street, and the Subway.

He was singing his way around Penang, and I rather liked his grin, so I felt sorry for him. I always hate to see a Yankee stranded in the Orient. It's no place for any kind of white man or white woman either.

"He'll be hopped with dope in a month," I thought. But I was wrong. When I saw him next, at Singapore, he was only thinner and his shoes were breaking through. A seedy man at a café piano. But he was good at the piano, and still grinning.

He was still grinning and pianoing when I saw him in Hue, and his feet were bare on the pedals. I gave him money for his grin, and he told me something of his story. All those beach combers have stories, but his was original, anyway, and his voice from New York was worth listening to.

He'd been on Tin Pan Alley back in the Town. "Words an' music," you know. But his stuff hadn't clicked and the girl friend had given him the air. So he'd come out East to find a fortune. When he found the fortune he'd go back to the Street and lay it in front of that girl.

Why does every poor devil who sails through the Suez Canal think he's going to light on a treasure in the Orient? I think it's Kipling's fault, and you can get mighty sick of Kipling when you're down and out on the China coast. The romance is washed out of you in a week, and you start to walk down the Lane of the Happy Pipes.

That was where the red-head was original. He wasn't washed out, and he said he *knew* he'd find a fortune. He said it with a look in his blue eyes that made me feel sorry for him, more. A chap with eyes like those would probably die a trying. It's easy to die on the China coast if you're thin and hungry to begin with.

Well, I offered him some money to start him to the States, and he wouldn't take it. So I started for the States, myself. I picked up this tramp ship Houri a few months later, out of Soc Trang, down in the Mekong's mouth. She was bound for Bangkok, and I hoped to catch a Messageries Maritimes liner out of Bangkok for the West.

I had a hundred crates of specimens waiting for me up there in Siam; I wanted to carry them to France and then hop over

*The old monk whispered on as the castaways listened.*

to America for a vacation. I didn't want to go to Bangkok on the Houri, but she was my only way.

**THE MINUTE** I boarded her at Soc Trang I knew she was in a pretty rotten way. If she was a Houri then a lot of Moslems are going to be disappointed in Paradise. With her rusty hull, warped decks, and skinny funnel spouting cumulus clouds, she looked the lousiest craft out of the South China Sea, and that's saying something.

Her fore deck was jammed with a mob of Malay pilgrims bound for some distant shrine of the Sakya Muni and led by a bag-o'-bones Buddhist monk who was nothing but a symbol of Asia. His begging bowl, shaved skull, bare arm and yellow robe were regulation enough, but he had a voice that must have been loaned him by a wizard. He stood in the middle of his Sunday School picnic excursion and prayed a chant that wrapped a tentacle around your soul.

A fine crowd of fellow passengers! Their incessant psalm-singing got under my hide the first thing, and I was already uneasy when the Houri sneaked out on the flood.

The cockney mate and the big Dutch skipper who showed me to my cabin made me uneasy, too. The cockney was a warty little runt whose face showed the wear of the China coast on a soul easily worn. The Dutch skipper looked like six-feet-five of sin with his mast-thick arms, hairy chest tattooed with anchors and angels, and a face of beefsteak lighted by eyes like buttons stuck in cups of jelly and boil-points on either cheek.

Somewhere I'd seen that Dutchman's face before, and it wasn't in the Colony Club at Saigon. Somewhere unpleasant.

I was wondering about it as the Houri trudged down a rose-colored evening sea with the coast of Cambodia lying off her starboard beam. I won't forget that evening. The Malays on the fore deck below the bridge where I stood were going through a set of evening devotionals that made the racket of a Southern camp-meeting sound tame. A gang of mighty tough-looking sailors were hanging in the rigging of the fore deck mast.

I was wondering where I'd seen the Dutch skipper's ugly face before, and vaguely glad of the 9-mm. Lüger automatic back in my cabin. It was a new gun and a beauty. But it never did me any good. Even as I thought of it a terrific roar tore out of the Houri's bowels. The dusk was full of smoke and screams and scarlet light. The deck jumped under my feet. I rammed my jaw a smash against a stanchion, and went spinning into the Gulf of Siam.

Then somebody had an arm around my neck, and I was being towed through bitter water. I caught a glimpse of the Houri riding down a swell like a drifting garden of flames. Something would burst in her middle and geysers of fire would shoot up from her deck.

The water was full of trash and junk. A pink-faced rat swam by and tried to climb on my head. When the Houri sank the sea became black as pitch under early night. I tried to swim, but my rescuer had me fast around the throat, and I couldn't seem to move my legs.

We were an eternity out there in the Gulf of Siam before a rush of breaking surf got a hold on us. Then we were heels over head in a churn of rolling sea. I went under again, and came to lying face-up on a strip of sand that seemed to be lost at the edge of the world.

A sick, round moon was sneaking out of a nest of green clouds, and the feeble rays disclosed a tiny beach backed by a steep bank of sand.

I caught a vague picture of my rescuer huddled over a mound of driftwood. Fire flickered in his cupped palms, and the wood began to blaze. Then he pivoted on his heel, and I saw his face. A grin under a stack of watery red hair. That Yankee kid I'd last seen beating a piano in Hue.

**I LET** a few quarts of the Gulf of Siam spill out of my mouth, and got up on unsteady knees.

"Where in the name of Joseph did you come from?" I managed. "Of all the—"

"Right off the boat," the musician chuckled, wringing water out of his cuffs. "Business went bad in Hue, an' I got me a job on that tramp ship. Was I broke? Say! Sold everything I owned except this suit an' this little pocket lighter my girl back in N'York once give me. Now it's come in handy. Say, that darned ship went up like a volcano. Smugglin' powder, she was. I was one of her crew. Workin' up her foremast, I was, when she blew. I seen you on the deck down there and I was gonna speak to you first chance I got. I seen you down there, and lucky I had my eye on you. When that first blast came you shot overboard like a high-dive champion. I went after you, sure as hell you were gone. Maybe you think there wasn't a riot aboard that ship! Wow! But I found you O.K.... Ash is my name, chief. Johnny Ash. Johnny to you, chief. You're that naturalist, ain't you? Yeh."

He grinned as I pumped his hand vigorously.

"That's O.K., chief," he said, as if he saved forty lives a day. "I—"

There was a scream. It came from out on the water and it echoed five times up the sand bank behind the beach. Johnny Ash went past me in a flying leap, dove into the surf, and was gone.

The moon crawled into a cloud and the only thing I could see was the patch of sand picked out by that handful of burning driftwood. Before I could decide to move my feet, Johnny Ash was back. Panting and blowing water, he strolled out of the combers.

When I saw what he carried in his arms I could have let out a yell. A marionette he carried; a skin-and-bones scarecrow with a face like a withered mangosteen—the Buddhist monk who had been leading that gang of pilgrims to a shrine up in Siam.

He laid the monk in the firelight, and we got to work.

"He was clingin' to a chunk of hatch cover out in the surf," Johnny Ash panted, working the monk's bony arms. "Goin' under and screamin' his lungs out. He fainted when I got him. Gee, he looks bad."

He looked just that. We emptied his lungs, flailed his arms and worked his legs, but we couldn't draw a breath out of him. His face was the color of old paper, his eyes squeezed shut, and his one-tooth mouth hung open like the mouth of a fish.

I gave him what first aid I knew, and then there was nothing to do but sit beside his inert frame. It wasn't pleasant to sit beside that huddle of skin and bones. The fire snapped, to cast dancy shadows down the narrow beach. The cliff behind the sand, the sky above, the Gulf of Siam were lost in a swirling, sceneless night. Our world was bounded by the reach of a smoky bonfire. It was the loneliest spot in the whole universe, right then.

Johnny Ash talked, because there was nothing else to do and no other place to go, while I thought dourly of my luggage and money sunk to the bottom of the Gulf. But I got snatches of what he said.

"The boat sank pretty fast. Most of the others got away, though. There were some lifeboats. We must 'a' come down pretty far on the tide. When the moon was up you couldn't see a thing out there on the water. Say, pal, this is real adventure, ain't it? You know, friend, I got a hunch I'm gonna find that fortune I once told you about. I been lookin' an' lookin'. I got a feelin' I'll hit it rich. Hit a fortune out here, see? Ever since I quit Broadway I've felt it, like. Queer, ain't it? Gee, I'd 'a' made good on Tin Pan Alley if I'd had a break. But your stuff has to be 'different' to click. Some new angle. New music. New lyric stuff. So I decided to leave the music world flat, see, an' chase up real dough. Somehow I got a hunch I'll find my treasure this trip—"

**THAT'S** the way the red-head chattered on while we dried ourselves around the fire and the monk was an unpleasant mummy on the sand. And you can believe it or not, but when Johnny Ash let out the words: "Got a hunch I'll find my treasure this trip—" that old bag-o'-bones monk suddenly sat up with a jerk that almost startled us over backward.

He sat up with a jump and a queer sigh; opened one milk-white eye and fastened it on Johnny Ash. I tell you it was weird. And maybe you think what he said didn't give that red-headed lad a nice shock.

"You shall find your fortune," he said in English. "Yes, *tuan*. By the oath of Buddhasatva next to come, you shall find a treasure out here. I will tell you how, *tuan*. I am dying, but before I die I tell you how. You saved me from the water bravely. You I shall reward, with a fortune."

I saw Johnny Ash's face go blank with surprise, and it got under my skin, too. But I shouldn't have been surprised at anything coming from a Buddhist monk. One of those apostles of Gautama had once argued Kant and John Stuart Mill and Monroe Doctrine with me in a lousy Yellow Sea backwater;

and I'd met another one who'd traveled the world around and could speak forty tongues and looked like a dried-up witch.

So I wasn't bowled over when the monk spoke English. It was the next thing he said which almost knocked me off my feet. He got a twig-like hand on Johnny Ash's arm, and his white eye glowed like a planet.

"I shall tell you how to find," he whispered, "the treasure of Buddha's Blue Cat—" And with that he fell back coughing.

I almost fell back coughing, myself. Buddha's Blue Cat! The treasure of Buddha's Blue Cat! Wow! You have heard of it if you've ever been east of DeLesseps's canal. They whisper of that treasure from Stamboul to the Shamu Desert. They talk of it with bated breath in the *serais* of Kokhand and in the taverns of Mozambique.

Every man and his brother who ever mapped a trail between Port Said and the Kuril Islands has heard of the porcelain image of Buddha's cat that sleeps in a Cambodian jungle with a fortune under its paws. They've probably tried a shot at it, too; and a good many of them never came back. Some said they died of fever in the jungle. Others said they disappeared; vanished from the face of the earth. Any Malay coolie or Annamite *pousse-pousse* boy would tell you they'd been eaten by the Blue Cat.

And the treasure was supposed to be still there, hiding around somewhere, unrifled! I knew any number of men who would give their ears to hear the first thing about the Blue Cat shrine. And here was this grisly old dying monk telling Johnny Ash he would show him how to gain the Blue Cat's gold. Lordy!

"For the Blue Cat guards the fortune with a secret one must know, *tuan*," his sepulchral voice was quavering on. "Thousands have never found the gold. Many more have failed with the treasure in their clasp. They did not know the secret. But I know it well, and will tell it to you, O *tuan* of the red hair. Because you save me I will reward you thus. Listen."

**JOHNNY ASH** listened, and I had my ears out stiff as tin. The

Yankee from New York and I crouched over that poor devil of a monk, and listened as if we were going to hear the secret of the universe.

The monk fixed his eye on the red-head's face, reared up on an elbow, and started a story. The fire snapped accompaniment. Wisps of wood-smoke wreathed about his shriveled skull. He had just the right atmosphere for his tale, and made the best of it.

Could he tell a story? Æsop and the garrulous Kalif of Ghand were tongue-tied compared to him. He was a troubadour and a minnesinger and an orator of acme degree, let me tell you. Waving a bony hand to shed queer shadows on the sand, he let his curious voice climb from alto to soprano, drop to bass and below, whisper weird as the winds in the lost caves of the Garo Hills as he chanted the legend of Buddha's Blue Cat.

Siddhartha Gautama (sang the monk) on becoming the Buddha, won the confidence of the people, and they all hastened to put their money in his keeping. This found him traveling through Cambodia with a bag of gold on his back bigger in size than Mount Langsho. Now the citizens of the countryside were outrageous thieves, and so troubled the Buddha he must needs rest himself under a banyan tree and figure out a way to bank his gold for good.

While meditating in the banyan's shade, he chewed the leaf of a lotus blossom and inspiration came. *Presto!* and he had conjured up a subterranean vault suitable for the storing of his enormous treasure. *Presto!* again, and he had called to his side a huge blue cat. Admonishing his cat to eat all and sundry who attempted to rob the vault, he mounted the cat at the cavern door to guard the fortune in gold.

Many had come, and the cat had not gone thin. In fact, it had grown big and fat. But alas! from sitting so long in the fierce Asian sunshine, the cat had gone blind. From crouching so long in one position it had petrified and turned into porcelain. Accordingly, it was sore as the devil at Buddha, and if the right person came along and did the right thing, the Blue Cat would tell a secret—show him how to get into the vault where the gold lay hidden.

That's the legend the skinny monk sang from his one-tooth mouth, and he sang it mighty well. Especially well did he sing of the gold in the cavern. Gold enough to make the hoardings of Midas the Phrygian and Croesus of Lydia look like the savings in the stocking of a fishmonger's wife by comparison. Gold nuggets and bars and *tikals* and beads and amulets all stuffed and sorted in bags. Bags of gold dust and bags of gold coin. Lordy!

He sang so well that Johnny Ash and I, stiff where we crouched, forgot we were lost on an unknown strip of beach. We forgot the monk was dying. We forgot everything. Our eyes were dazzled by visions of a cave stuffed with a fortune in gold; and when the ancient monk told us the Blue Cat shrine was not so far from where we'd landed on that beach, we almost fell on our faces.

**"SO THE BLUE CAT** sits in the jungle at the door of a little shrine," the old monk whispered on. "And it is not far from this beach, *tuan*. There is a village named Lua Kapong. The shrine of the Blue Cat is near the village. Not far away. Look you, *tuan*. This beach I know well. Years ago I sat praying on this very bit of sand. Behind us stands a cliff. There is a trail up the cliff. Yes. A trail leading to Lua Kapong where sits the Blue Cat. I can smell it, *tuan*. I know. The Blue Cat is near. It is not far—to Lua Kapong."

Lordy! Johnny Ash was making sounds in his throat. My mouth seemed full of sawdust. Before the monk could say more a spasm of coughing tortured his withered body. Blood bubbles floated from his lips. He must have been hurt internally, for the coughing turned his face grass-green, reared him on his elbows and poised him, gasping. Then he sank back with a whistly sigh.

I tell you, it was shivery on that little beach with the moon gone out and the dark closing in, blue-black, and the smoky fire crackling to send macabre shadows flitting down the sand.

"Listen!" squawked the monk with sudden strength. *"Tuan* of the red hair, you who saved me from the watery death—listen, *tuan.* Go you to the shrine of the Blue Cat. Mark well these words: *Give the cat a right eye that can see,* and the cat will point the way to find the gold! When you find the gold, *do right."*

The dying man coughed so hard you could almost hear his bones rattle. When he spoke again his voice was a whisper's echo.

"Do you remember. Give the cat a right eye that can see! Find gold! Do—do right." His voice was a croak. "I die now. *Tabay, tuan—"*

His lips moved, but no voice came. His lips grinned. His eyes clamped shut. His cheeks sank into purple wells; body flattened into the sand; mouth yawned open. The solitary tooth glittered bleakly in the shifty fireglow. The monk was dead.

Johnny Ash looked at me; his voice struggling out of a white mouth. "Bradshaw! You heard what this guy said? Did you hear him, pal? Do you get it? A cavern cram full o' gelt! A fortune! I knew it, pal! I knew I'd hit a fortune out here. Wow! A cave stuffed with gold an' nothin' to stop you takin' it save a cat made outa crockery."

And a few other things. I saw them, and let out a startled yell. The red-headed kid jumped around fast, but he wasn't in time to see what I saw. They were gone when he looked; but I'd seen them, no mistake.

The sweat crawled out on my forehead, and I glared at the wedge of brushwood masking the foot of the sand bank where it dropped behind the beach. The light from our expiring bonfire just reached those bushes and made hot coals of the six pairs of eyes in the six faces I had seen peering through the undergrowth.

**SIX FACES** like a row of devil-masks hanging in the brush!

Six faces with open mouths and burning eyes, distorted from the effort to listen!

The first four faces I didn't recognize. But the last two I knew. One was hook-beaked, scabby, leering—the face of the cockney mate of the ill-fated Houri. The last in line was a slice of beef-steak, sin-pocked and grinning, with piggy, lusting eyes and flamy boil-heads atop each high cheekbone. The face of the Houri's big Dutch skipper!

Nor was that all. The cockney had a hand up under his chin, and in that hand was a knife that gleamed like a giant needle, catching straying beams from the fire. And the Dutchman had a fist to part the bushes, and in that fist was a monster automatic.

That wasn't all, either. The minute I saw the Dutch skipper's face, this time, I remembered where I'd seen it before. A poster in the police bureau at Singapore. That grin above the salient legend: "Dirk van Deventer. Wanted for murder." No wonder I let loose a howl.

Johnny Ash spun around as I yelled, and the faces vanished. I got a hand on the red-head's arm.

"Did you see 'em?" I gasped. "In the bushes over there. They must 'a' seen our fire from where they landed farther up the beach, and sneaked up on us. Six of them. The skipper and the mate from the Houri. And four others."

"The crew! There were only five of us workin' the deck—"

"Yes! Hiding there in the bushes. You get it? They hid in those bushes and overheard everything that monk told you about the Blue Cat. And the mate carried a knife while the Dutchman had a gun."

Johnny Ash stood stunned. Then he made a dive for the underbrush, with me after him. I rather expected a burst of automatic fire would greet our charge, but nothing happened. We thrashed into the bushes and couldn't find a single human being.

We found tracks, though. Those six had sneaked out quiet

as a troop of tigers, but they'd left a trail. I snatched a torch out of the bonfire and looked over the ground.

Footprints in the damp sand showed where the crowd had hidden, and marched away to a path mounting the bank behind the beach. It didn't take any little bird to tell me where those six mariners were heading.

As I stood staring at the footprints, the red-head's hand smote me hard between the shoulder blades.

"Come on, brother!" he hollered. His blue eyes blazed behind a tossing sheaf of carroty hair. His words came shrill with excitement. "Let's get goin', pal. We're off. We're goin' to Lua Kapong—

With that, he sprinted up the sandy trail. The gold rush had begun!

## CHAPTER II

# THE BLUE CAT

LUA KAPONG IS not a village. It is not. It is a smell. It smells like a *durian*, which is an Oriental fruit smelling worse than those little bombs American urchins throw on Halloween night.

A bilious, sluggish river crawls seaward through a jungle suffering from gangrene; and where the stream squirms clear of the trees, it spews broad mud banks. Lua Kapong chooses to squat on the mud banks.

A scribble of native huts perched high atop poles, looking for all the world like queer birds stalking across the muck. A *cul-de-sac* of nasty Chinese bungalows. A scatter of European sheds abandoned to spiders. A backwater alive with flopping crocodiles and the stink of dead fish. A tropic sunshine sucking skyward evil steam to sour the local air. A decaying wharf, a decaying oil tank, a decaying hotel run by a decayed Leo Restoul, *propriétaire*.

What a place! When I saw that Asian garden spot, I suffered no doubts about the dying Buddhist monk smelling its inland trail from the beach.

I give you my word, I never wanted to go there. I wasn't anxious to join a fortune hunt with four tramp sailors led by ruffians armed with knife and gun—fellows who looked capable of stabbing their mothers for a plugged franc, and grinning while they did it—whereas I was armed with nothing but malaria. Furthermore, the Blue Cat shrine had proved a fatal monkey-business for some of the toughest adventurers down the China coast.

The more I thought about it, the less I liked the idea. The monk had said he'd give away the secret to the treasure; but what had he given away? As far as I could figure, he'd handed out nothing but a lot of Oriental epigrams. "Give the cat a right eye that can see. Find gold. Do right." What did that rot mean? All very illuminating.

But the red-headed Johnny Ash had started for Lua Kapong at top speed, and there was nothing I could do but follow. He'd saved my life, so I had to stick by him.

I chased him up the trail and we plugged off through the jungle side by side. He wasn't going to let any six men or any sixty men rob him of his fortune, and you can't talk to a Yankee with red hair and gold in his soul at the same time.

We got to Lua Kapong just as the sun was climbing like a blazing chariot wheel out of the East. Johnny Ash spied the decaying hotel down by the river's edge; raced me through the steaming *cul-de-sac* right up to the hotel's sick veranda.

A score of *kra* monkeys were cluttering on the veranda roof; a lemon-faced house boy snored on the front step; and a man with a face like a Christmas pudding leaned in the dowdy doorway. This was Leo Restoul, *propriétaire*. A pudgy, corpulent Frenchman spoiling in that tropic backwater.

Johnny Ash, who had some coins in his belt, hired a room and dashed indoors to look around. I stayed for a talk with Monsieur Restoul.

You understand, I had no use for this treasure hunt affair. And I'd conceived a bright idea. There would be river boats bringing mail up to Lua Kapong, and I'd get Johnny Ash away on the first river boat along, before the bullet or blade of a competitor dodged into his reckless head. The red-head had saved my life, and it was up to me to save his.

**BUT THE** Frenchman laughed soprano when I asked him if the Messageries Fluviales steamed through to Lua Kapong. River boats! But, *Sacré Dieu!* The mail boat had left only yesterday. There would not be another one along for three months. The only way out of Lua Kapong was an overland trek through the jungle—a hundred hard-fought miles to Kampot, the nearest port away.

The Frenchman laughed when he told me the news. I could have punched his nose. I had even made a fist, when Johnny Ash danced out of the door, caught my arm, and led me into the hotel.

Inside there was a smoky room fouled with tables, slinky mongrel dogs, an American bar under a broken electric fan shrouded in cobwebs. Six figures were hunched at a corner table, and six faces grinned at my entry.

And there I was, with the red-head; marooned in the middle of a treasure hunt.

Well, nothing happened for a week. (Things started to happen on the eighth day, though, you can bet your life on that!) But the first week was full of nothing save apprehension, malaria, and daily trips out to the shrine of the famous Blue Cat.

The path to the shrine started at the other edge of town; wandered through a grove of *kaladang* into deep jungle. Across marshy, dankish fens where rags of mist held fever over stagnant pools. Through thatches of clumpy bamboo, batches of lime and cycas. Down a ravine choked with vines and rotting trees covered with fungi.

Like an artery into the very heart of Asia that path led, bringing up finally to a wall of shale that jutted abruptly out of the trees. A steep wall of shale that made a fence to a region of hills which rolled off eastward beyond the jungle, rugged where the sun would rise.

At the base of this cliff grew a forest of *mohors* where monkeys swung; and the Blue Cat sat under a banyan tree. The banyan was old as sin, digging a thousand gnarled fingers into the moss about its many roots; and the Blue Cat crouched facing a little Buddhist shrine scooped into that cliff of shale.

The shrine in the cliff was some three feet deep and nine feet high, its floor paved with flat green stone, its interior walled and roofed with panels of eaglewood that must have been carved when Buddha's wife was still wondering if he'd ever come home.

Stones, cobwebs and moss dripped through the fusty wood of the shrine's ceiling, but the wooden back wall was intact, dead with great age, stained dull. I've seen some pretty smart pieces of carving in my day, but I've never seen wood wrought in the fashion of that paneled back wall.

Hundreds of tiny figures, figurines, knobs, paradigms, flowers and symbols were cut in intricate pattern across the panel, worked in an intricate design that would have made shamefaced the cabinet-makers and wood-carvers of the Middle Ages. Impossible to describe the thing. It was a design to make your eyes water.

**THE PORCELAIN** cat was something wonderful, too. Only in Asia can you find such a thing. Mystery? The East knows how to brew one for you at every turn. That image sitting silent and calm in the heart of a jungle a million miles from nowhere was one of Asia's weirdest jobs. It would have taken modern sculptors three generations to fashion such a thing, and forty engineers, an army of workmen and a modern railroad to set it up there in the jungle.

A cat *couchant,* stretched out lazy on a marble pedestal, arched back some ten feet above ground, and thirty feet long from its tail to the paws curled under its chin. What a cat! And made of cobalt-blue, chinalike porcelain that must have been fired in the furnace of a master ceramist. And invented in the mind of a maniac.

You know the Chinese love for the bizarre. You know their images. That cat was covered with scrolls and little horns, knobules and cornices; grinned a mouth full of scissory teeth, fiercely, in a face of incredible design; and stared with eyes like empty saucers at the shrine in the shale cliff. That was the Blue Cat.

And right there in front of the Blue Cat, standing in awe and with nerves tingling, Johnny Ash and I were checkmated.

"We aren't going to find any fortune," I reminded, "or even a smell of one until we figure out what the monk's dying words meant. Give the cat a right eye that can see. Maybe you can do it, Ash, but I confess I'm no surgeon. And I don't like fooling with this cat, I can tell you. A lot of boys have come out here hunting gold and never been heard of again. Besides, we've got those six criminals from your boat to contend with."

Johnny Ash stood fingering his jaw, trying to puzzle out the monk's tricky sentence. He examined the right eye of the Blue Cat, which was just like the blank eye in any other image. Then he examined the Blue Cat from stem to stern. After which we went over every inch of the ground under the banyan, and finished up inspecting the shrine.

A few lizards crawled around to stare at us. Juicy spiders scuttled down the wood panels walling the shallow shrine. Our inspection resulted us nothing.

"I've got a certain feeling," I told my companion, "that six ugly sailor-men are hiding in the bushes around here and watching us the way cats watch sparrows. Maybe it's a good thing we aren't finding the door to any Aladdin's Cave. Listen,

Ash. We better give up this nonsense, and make tracks out of town. I don't like it here a little bit."

"I don't, either," he grinned. "But that monk said there was gold hanging around, an' I'm gonna get it if anybody does."

We didn't get it that day. We got nothing except sunburn. The same on the following day, although I'd sat up all night with a sweet dose of fever, and Johnny Ash sat up all night trying to figure out the monk's little puzzle.

First thing in the morning we went out to the Blue Cat for another look at its problematical eye. Other visitors had beaten us to it. We found the tracks, but no other sign of them. Johnny Ash spent the morning staring at the porcelain image, and I spent the morning waiting for a bullet to buzz out of somewhere and knock me down.

**THE SAME** for the third and fourth days, and no results. And the affair began to wear on my nerves. Those strolls through the jungle were no May walks to begin with. Never in my life had I heard a place as quiet as that jungle was. I've been lost alone on the desert of Oman and tramped the forgotten hills of the Hindu Kush, and I thought those places were quiet. But they were shouting market-squares compared to that rank jungle where the Blue Cat crouched.

The stillness in there was thick as steam. Monkey gabble only emphasized the quietude. Snakes slipping out of black pools made a noise. It got under one's hide.

And then there were those six lousy ruffians from the Houri. They sneaked around the hotel with grins on the side of their mouths, giving Johnny Ash and me shrewd glances, whispering among themselves, stealing off by themselves through the town, watching. Watching. Always watching.

They watched us, and we watched them—each waiting for the other to make a move. Remembering the cockney's knife and the Dutchman's automatic, I didn't like the game at all. Six against two, and the Dutchman had already given himself a name for homicide.

The thing almost had a humorous angle. We all lived together in Leo Restoul's scabby hotel; ate together in the same room. The seamen ate at one end of the room; Ash and I enjoyed our rice and wine at the other.

We watched, I repeat, the sea dogs; they watched us. The skipper and the mate bossed the others of their crew; and I have every good reason to remember those four deck hands. One was a Russian with a Nihilist's beard and a rum-blossom nose. One was a swart Spaniard with brass rings dangling from enormous ears. One was a Senegambian black; face darker than anthracite, tattooed lips split in a monstrous watermelon grin. One was a Scotsman with a livid scar bisecting his mouth and Chinese eyes under sandy brows.

Johnny Ash coolly told me they had been a tough crowd in a forecastle, and they looked twice as tough out of one. Put them altogether and they didn't spell "mother," by any means.

"Don't worry," I said. "Every time we sneak out to that Blue Cat, they sneak out and watch us. They keep a man posted there all night, I can bet. Look here, Ash. It would be a swell stunt if we cleared out of Lua Kapong. We're almost out of the few coins we had in our pants. We better hit overland before some snake decides to strike."

I said that more than once. The red-head's reply never varied. He would take out his pocket lighter and start the tiny flame. "The girl who give me this is waiting for me to bring her back a fortune. I'm gonna find one out here. The monk fixed it up—gave us the dope."

"Gave us hell," I would say. "Dumped us down in the middle of a jungle backwater in the midst of a treasure hunt with a gang of escaped murderers. We'd be wise to clear out. Who can figure the monk's lingo, anyhow? We all squat around that hotel like a lot of ninnies, foreheads wrinkled, eyes blank in thought, brains churning. Trying to get the meaning of a fool yellow mendicant's puzzle-problem."

"I'll find that fortune," was all he would concede.

And for a whole week we discovered no cavern jammed with gold, or anything else of value. For a week nothing happened. Then the eighth day the Russian sailor vanished and was never heard of again.

CHAPTER III

# DEATH AND THE EYE

**IT WAS THE** Spaniard who started asking the whereabouts of Bonstamski, the Russian, early afternoon of the day the Slav vanished. That started the negro and the Scotsman going, and they asked the cockney mate and the Dutch skipper.

When the Russian didn't turn up at twilight the Dutch skipper came over to ask Ash and me about it. It was the first time any of that crowd had spoken to us in Lua Kapong. He simply asked in a gentle Dutch voice if we'd seen the Russian. We gently advised we had not.

By midnight the whole native quarter was out searching. It's not so easy for a man to vanish from an isolated community. But friend Slav might have dissolved into thin smoke. His sailor friends looked scared. I was mystified. Johnny Ash said nothing. Leo Restoul raved because the man had paid nothing on his bill, and said:

"*Parbleu!* There is a shrine near here called the Blue Cat. Those who go near it are eaten by the image. That is so. It has happened before. Those fools. They come here hunting gold; expecting to see it lying around. I tell them there is no gold. They stay. They hunt. Then one day they vanish. Without paying the bill!"

As if we did not know!

The Scotsman with Oriental eyes was next. Johnny Ash and I spent the day inspecting the shrine and mulling over the monk's puzzle. I knew the Dutchman and his gang were watching us; I could hear them in the tall grass under the *mohors*. If they watched us they didn't see anything.

And that night the Scotch beach comber wasn't to be found. The big negro and the Spaniard, the Dutchman and the cockney hunted high and low, through the town and into the jungle. Leo Restoul hunted. Johnny Ash and I wondered.

None of the natives had seen the man since noon. *Mynheer* the skipper claimed he'd left the Scotch beggar sitting on the hotel veranda. The Spanish brigand said he'd last seen the Scotty strolling off through the *kaladangs*. It was all very queer.

"Say," Johnny Ash pointed out to me that night. "You suppose them guys could have found gold and beat it with the treasure?"

"Not on your life!" I told him. "That Dutchman keeps one of his men watching the next one all the time. Either he or his cockney mate is out watching the shrine all the time, too; I've decided that from what the hotel keeper, here, tells me. The Dutchman and cockney are only in the hotel together at meal time, see? Then, either one or the other goes away somewhere. To the Blue Cat, if I know anything. And you can bet they keep an eye on those sailors. Then how could that Russian and this Scotch fellow have disappeared? Don't ask me. But let me tell you. You heard what the Frenchman said about it? Me, I'm all for getting out of here before one of *us* does a vanishing act."

"You mean start a tramp overland?"

"You bet your life, kid. I'm fed up on this fortune hunt."

"I'll find the fortune!" he grinned. "I know I will. I'll hit it before those other devils do, that's sure. Just gimme time."

Time! Nine days in a steaming tropic hole. Nine days in an out-of-the-world jungle, glaring at a porcelain idol. Nine days in a frowzy hotel, being watched and watching, striving over an idiotic little puzzle that might mean anything or nothing whatever. I tell you, I was sick to death of it. Two men had apparently been wiped off the picture. Who would be next?

The big Senegambian negro was next!

He made it three in a row. His footsteps could be trailed,

though. They walked up the path leading to the Blue Cat and disappeared under the banyan tree.

I could hear the Dutchman talking about it to the cockney and the Spaniard on the veranda that evening. Ash and I were in the hotel. The three on the veranda sounded pretty scared.

The Dutchman told the Spaniard to go out to the Blue Cat and stay there all night in hiding, to see if either Ash or I showed up at the shrine. The red-head and I overheard that plan, and we stayed in our room all night.

At times we could hear either the Dutchman or the cockney talking with the French hotel keeper on the veranda below. All night they kept at it. In the morning, the Dutch skipper showed up with a pallid face and something like terror in his eyes. The cockney was looking pretty green around the gills, too.

The Spaniard—the last of their crew—had disappeared; vanished under the banyan tree during the night. Johnny Ash gave me the news; said the fat Frenchman had given it to him.

"**THAT** Spig is gone, too," the red-head informed me over our morning coffee, behind the closed blinds of our room. "You heard 'em send him out to the shrine las' night. Well, the cockney went out lookin' fer him this mornin', an' he wasn't to be found anywhere. Say, if this keeps up we won't have any competition at all—"

"Ash!" I said, getting him by the collar. "I'm through. I know the Orient better than you ever will. Something happened to those four sailors that isn't on the books! They're dead as hell, or I miss my guess. And so will you and I be, if we stick on this fool job. That monk handed out a lot of trash, and it's just lucky we weren't the ones to get it in the neck. Now we're going to clear out of town. To hell with the Blue Cat!"

I was mad clean through, and about as scared as I ever hope to be. Something was doing out there near that shrine. Something had done away with those four tough sailors, and I wasn't going to stand by until it did away with me.

Besides, I was getting up to my neck in malaria, sick of the vile hotel fare, and sick of hearing the red-head trying to solve the monk's Oriental puzzle.

"We've wasted eleven days in those rotten jungles and this lousy hole. We haven't come across a sign of gold. Now we're going to wash our hands of it all. Our money's gone and we'll have to sneak out. Have to sneak, anyway. If that Dutchman and his pal spotted us leaving town they might think we'd found the gold, and try to knock us off. I'm for fighting with nobody. You get me, Ash? We're going out of here to-night—"

All day I argued with him about it, and at sunset he broke down. I guess the vanishing of the four sailors wasn't sitting too well on his stomach, either. Our hide-and-seek with the Blue Cat and the ruffians from the Houri was too nerve-tweaking for even a song writer from New York City.

So we crept out of the hotel just at dusk, without the French-man seeing us go; pocketed a few provisions, spending our last *piastre* at a Chinese trader's in the middle of the *cul-de-sac;* and turned our steps for the trail by the river.

Neither the cockney nor the Dutch giant had been in the hotel when we left, and we were confident of making a get-away. I knew the red-headed kid was sick with disappointment, and I didn't say anything. I, myself, would have enjoyed stumbling across a fortune in gold, had it been there for the stumbling. It wasn't going to be any fun to trek down the river broke and beat a trail back to Saigon like a penniless tramp.

I was thinking of the world in no dulcet terms as we thread-ed our way through the *cul-de-sac* of the town, heading for the riverside.

"Curse the Houri for a boat," I said to myself. "Curse the Blue Cat!"

As I said that, Johnny Ash made a grab at my sleeve and yanked me into the shadows of an evil-smelling mud hutch. Out of sight just in time! The lane we'd been treading had been deserted to mongrel dogs, mud, and mist wreathing up from the river. Now a man had popped out of an alley, and, keeping in shadow, hustled up the lane ahead of us.

"The cockney!" Johnny Ash whispered.

The words weren't off his lips before a second man darted from the alley and flitted down the shadowy lane, hard on the heels of the little mate. There was stealth in the movement of this second man. Like a stalking gorilla. And when I realized who he was, ten shivers trickled up my spine. That was the big Dutch skipper.

A fat round moon was just riding up into the sky, and the lane was full of blue shades and pallid light. The cockney walked nervously, fast. The Dutchman flickered in and out of shadow.

"Come on!" Johnny Ash breathed wildly. "Something's up now. That runt in the lead is headin' for the path to the Blue Cat."

The cockney ducked up a narrow byway. The Dutchman followed the cockney. Johnny Ash and I followed him.

IT WAS lonely down in that end of town. Most of the natives lived on the mud near the old French hotel and spent their early evenings gambling away their shirts in the Chinese quarter.

Here were abandoned sheds and shanties, rambly empty bungalows and shacks that had once housed Europeans avid after petroleum and tin. The Europeans had gone, and their works were not standing up against the hand of Asia. Sheds and shacks leaned broken with decay; peopled with nothing but ghosts. A gloomy district.

Where the village ended on the edge of jungle stood a sheet-iron warehouse, dilapidated and empty. The Dutchman caught the cockney just as he reached the warehouse. The cockney voiced a squawk of dismay; there was a brief, violent struggle; then the big Dutchman dragged his captive through the ware-house door.

With nerves ajangle, Johnny Ash and I crept down the lane and stole on tiptoe up to the warehouse. Creeping along the rusty iron wall, we could hear clearly the cockney's dolorous whine:

"Now Dirk! Don't! Ow! Yer gonna kill me? Wait! Wait, ol' man! Ow! Yer chokin'! Lay off, Dirk! What's it yuh wanna me—attackin' me like a bloomin' thug!"

A harsh laugh sounding like the rattle of nails in a brass bucket drifted from a window cut in the iron wall above my head. The harsh cacophony snapped quiet the cockney's whine; and brought a mist out on my forehead.

Once before I had heard a similar laugh. One afternoon I'd seen a colonial soldier yank his revolver to shoot down a baby orang-outang which had been squealing in a tree overhead and annoying his siesta. The monkey's mother had dashed off with the corpse, squalling in anguish. Her cry would have torn the heart of a Kameroon witch doctor, but that soldier had guffawed.

It was just such a laugh as the Dutchman in the shed managed to give. The cockney gurgled out a wail of fear. Followed the sound of scuffling. Was the skipper murdering his mate in cold blood?

Sweating, Johnny Ash and I raised our heads; moved to a position which commanded a view through the little window. The bright moon was high and the lane beside the shed was lighted with moonshine. This made our station at the window more than hazardous; but it also afforded us a picture of what went on in the warehouse, for a shaft of yellow beams washed down through a hole rotted in the roof and served to illuminate the barn.

The Dutchman had the cockney backed against a wall; his massive hands fastened on the limey's wrists; a brutal knee driven into the limey's stomach to pin him fast.

From the window the Dutchman's face could not be seen; but moonbeams picked out the cockney's countenance in bold relief. The little mate wasn't leering like a tough, now. You bet he wasn't.

His eyes were glowing with fear; his raffish mouth twisting with pain. He seemed to be clutching something precious in his captured fists; and sweat dripped down his cheeks as if his temples had been melting butter.

"Let us stop the foolishness, *ja!*" the Dutchman was growling. "I haff no time now to waste. Come, little friend. You haff been double crossing your old skipper, eh? So! I know it. Last night I sent you to watch the Blue Cat, *ja.* And back you came with three gold pieces in your fist, eh? You hid them in the belt you haff. You did not guess I was every night searching your belt, eh? So. Where did you get the gold? How did you get into the treasure vaults and where are they found, eh? Tell me, little roach, or by the bones of Peter van der May, I will twist your throat until your neck breaks! Tell me!"

**MAYBE** you think that speech of the Dutchman's didn't have the two of us at the window staring pop-eyed. The little cockney was squirming, impaled on the wall by his captor's knee; his voice burbling in his neck. Seeing murder in the Dutchman's eye, no doubt, he exhaled a howl.

"Wait. I weren't gonna double cross you, Dirk. Honest to Gawd, I weren't."

How the Dutchman laughed.

"You ain't gonna, now, anyhows. It iss all so funny. I was leaving you live last of all, because I never guess you'd haff the brain to figure out the secret of what that old monk said." (Johnny Ash and I sweated chill water when we heard those words, believe me!)

"*Nein!* I did not guess you would learn the puzzle, my friend. Ho, ho! That you wass smarter than us all. A joke. So! I kill those others one by one and hide their bodies in the banyan tree to get them out of the way. Later I should kill you, eh? Why should I divide any treasure with five others, ha? But I leave the two fool Yankees live because Yankees are smart. They, I think, will be the ones who figure out the puzzle. I watch them do it and then take the prize away from them. Never would I guess it wass you who would get first to the gold. Come, then. How did you get the gold and where? You tell me now or I kill you so. *Ja!*"

He twisted the cockney's wrist. The cockney yowled; and something happened. His tortured hand flew open and three gold coins jingled on the dirt floor at his feet. I saw them. The red-head beside me saw them. The Dutch skipper saw them. He screamed a red hot curse when he saw them, too.

Three gold coins. Gold! Three little golden disks glinting dully in the moonlight.

Then something else happened. The laughing giant of a skipper gave a sudden wrench on his captive's other wrist. The fingers of that hand spread open, and another object rolled, flashing, across the dirt. What do you think it was? A *pocket mirror!*

The legs almost gave out under me as the monk's words darted through my mind. "Give the cat a right eye that can see!" A pocket mirror!

Johnny Ash started to whisper, but he didn't have time. *Mynheer* the skipper had snatched up the mirror, caught at the little mate's throat, and sent him spinning across the floor.

"Ho-ho!" the Dutchman snarled. "So that is the eye! Come then, my friend. You will take me to the Blue Cat and show how it works. You will take me to the gold." He launched a kick at the cockney's spine, and the miserable little man let out a cry of anguish.

"Take me now, limey. And no tricks, *nein*. You try to fool Dirk van Deventer, again, and I will snap your neck in two, see? Quick! I am impatient. Let us go!"

## CHAPTER IV

# TO THE TREASURE!

**ARM IN ARM** the pair tramped out of the warehouse and started up the path through the *kaladangs*. They passed within thirteen inches of the place where the red-head and I crouched hiding in the weeds.

Lucky for us, the Dutchman didn't see us there. Bad business if the big skipper had spotted us just then. He had his automatic clamped in his fist, and the expression on his face as he stalked by was not nice to see.

My heart was banging all over my chest as I got to my toes, and, scuttling where the steamy shadows clung, went after them. Johnny Ash was white-faced, but he wore a grin, and his blue eyes sparkled. He looked a little mad with the moonbeams in his red hair. I must have been a little mad, myself, or I'd never have gone up that jungle path.

If that jungle was bad enough in daylight it was villainous at night. The lush roof of foliage defied the moonlight and spread a mantle of darkness that seemed to sweat in the torpid heat. Snarling roots, capsicum brush and gluey mud made traveling a contest.

The jungle didn't want visitors that night. It wanted to belch and steam without human intervention, and it fought like the devil to stay and betray the progress of our boots.

Only the racket made by the two in the lead saved our following feet from being heard. Van Deventer's pungent curses and the little mate's shrill cockney oaths spit out a continuous clamor. The Dutchman would yell for more speed and wrench his captive's arm. The cockney would squall in pain. The Dutchman would laugh his scarlet laugh.

That was a murderer's laugh, and I never wanted it to presage my own funeral. It didn't seem to bother Johnny Ash. It was all I could do to keep that red-head behind me and quiet.

The path seemed to wander for miles that night. The jungle was hot, but I was chilled with sweat when the shale cliff appeared as a moonlit shadow above the treetops, and the pair in front gained the *mohor* forest.

The trees weren't so thick in there. Pools of yellow moonlight lay on the moss below the vine-clad limbs. Rags of malarial mist wandered like wraiths among the tree trunks.

If ever I saw a rendezvous for ghosts, that moon-illuminated grove of *mohor* trees was one. Only the men hustling up the trail ahead weren't ghosts. One was a wretched little vagabond with the taste of death in his mouth. The other was a giant Hollander with gold-lust in his soul, a godless laugh in his black teeth, and predatory hands anxious to claw at a treasure.

**WHEN** they reached the clearing where the Blue Cat crouched under the ancient banyan directly beneath the cliff's frown, Van Deventer yanked his victim to a halt, and the red-head and I dropped flat in a tangle of underbrush.

The worthy mariners stood at the head of the porcelain image. Johnny Ash and I were not fifteen feet away. For a moment the Dutchman growled in hoarse undertone. During the interval the red-head spraddled tense at my elbow stuck his hand under my chin and tilted my face upward.

"Look," he whispered softly. "Overhead. In the upper branches of that banyan. Above the cat."

The moon was a canary-yellow wafer behind the tangle of gnarly limbs, and etched with faint light the outlines of the four things roosting in the topmost branches. Black against the sky they hung, and at first I thought they were buzzards.

Buzzards! Sweat poured out on my face. I remembered the Dutchman's words, spoken in the warehouse. I hadn't quite caught them, then, but I caught their meaning now.

Slowly the four dangling figures turned, swinging on cords that hung them by the neck. The Russian, the Negro, the

Scotchman, the Spaniard. Van Deventer had killed them, and hung them high in the banyan tree to hide!

I think I gasped like a radiator valve, for Johnny Ash slapped a hand across my mouth.

"Watch 'em, pal. The cockney—"

I turned my gaze from the horrid sight in the tree in time to glimpse the Dutchman and the cockney duck into the shrine scooped out of the cliff base. Like a spotlight turned on a stage, the moon sent a shaft of beams slanting into that shallow shrine. The two stood facing the back wall, the cockney running his fingers over the lacy woodwork.

As I watched pop-eyed, the back wall swung inward with a senile moan. Dutchman and cockney disappeared. The wooden panel hissed back into place.

"Come on!" snarled Johnny Ash, and we crept close.

I give you my word, I didn't want to go on. I didn't like that soundless jungle. I didn't like those four cadavers hanging in the uppermost branches of the banyan against the tropic moon. I didn't like the diabolical china cat with the pocket mirror set into its right eye.

"Give the cat a right eye that can see," had said the monk, "and the cat will point the way to the treasure." The cockney mate of the Houri had guessed out the problem. That little mirror—obviously filched from Leo Restoul's scabby hotel— gleamed like an optic in the cat's preposterous porcelain face.

And pointed the way to the treasure!

Johnny Ash and I stared like fools. The porcelain image faced the shrine in the cliff, and the looking-glass set into the right eye of that image mirrored a tiny portion of the shrine's back wall; picked out a section of the involved and intricate diagram carved in the wooden panel.

Never in the world could one have found it, otherwise. But by looking in the mirror one could see it as solutions make easy what seems a difficult trick. An arrow, carved in the wood, pointing to a little wooden lever.

I tell you, it was ingenious. The red-head flung around from the face of the porcelain cat and leaped into the shrine. But I was standing in the way of the mirror, and he couldn't find that carved arrow to save his soul. It had melted into the pattern; seemed to vanish.

The mirror, you see, made it seem to appear in that section of the carved paneling where it wasn't. He snapped on his pocket-lighter and fumbled over every inch of the wall. Only then did we realize we must watch the mirror in the cat's eye, watch the reflected picture, and move our hand until the mirror showed it on the arrow.

Have you ever tried looking over your shoulder into a mirror and attempting to place your finger on a reflected object? That was the trick. Stare straight at the wall of the shrine and your gaze was lost in a confusion of Chinese patterns.

My mind was on that gibbet of a banyan tree and the Dutchman who had made it so. But Johnny Ash's mind was all for finding the arrow in the panel, and he found it. His finger touched the tiny lever, and a portion of the panel swung inward. He gave a laugh as the panel swung to reveal a yawning tunnel mouth that bored like a hallway leading deep down to hell.

**A STALE** breath of fetid, dank air whispered out of the tunnel and stirred my hair. A smell like the smell of an opened tomb. Age-lain dust coiled up in the wind and a thousand disturbed ghosts from vanished yesterdays went whispering down the dark-hung tunnel walls.

"Gosh!" ejaculated Johnny Ash. "If the wise guys back on Tin Pan Alley could only see this! Gee!" he grabbed my hand. "Come along. Get goin'!"

"Do I look crazy?" I rasped. He might well have said I did! "You think I'm going down that tunnel after a man who's just murdered four sailors and is wanted over in Malaya for a fifth murder? And we haven't got a weapon on us."

"I'm going down there," the red-head growled. "That monk said I'd find a fortune in here, an' I'm the guy who's gonna get it. To hell with that Dutchman! Who's afraid of a gun? He can't see us in the dark. Come on, brother, and get your share!"

I was afraid of a gun and made haste to confess the fact. But I went on just the same, and I got my share. You bet I did. More than my share! But I wasn't going to let that fool song writer from New York go first, and he wasn't going to go last. So we traveled side by side.

The red-head let the panel swish back into place; then he snapped on that infernal little lighter his girl safely home in New York had given him, and left it standing at the base of the wooden door.

"This tunnel may branch off, an' that light'll come in handy, in case we have to locate the exit in a hurry," he suggested with great cheer. "All ready, pal. Say, it *is* black as pitch, ain't it?"

Blacker than pitch. The feeble, puerile blaze of the lighter died out hastily as we fumbled our way down that subterranean corridor. Soon we edged around a turn, and Stygian darkness closed in behind us. Lordy! was it dark?

And everywhere that fusty smell of age, rot, long-lying dust. The dust was a real enemy, too. It clouded under our sneaking feet and kept me in constant nervous fear of a nasal explosion. A good old-fashioned sneeze in that situation might have meant a ticket to Paradise. Impossible to tell how far the Dutchman and cockney were in the lead. It made my spine shiver to think of them.

If I've ever done anything foolhardy in my life it was the time I crept down that hall of midnight, trailing that armed Dutch assassin. And the only weapon urging me on was the fear that a red-skulled jazz hound from New York would think me craven. Wow!

Perhaps the tunnel meandered for a mile. Perhaps ten thousand miles. I, myself, think I crept through that blind and perilous darkness for a score of æons. Every forward step had the heart bounding under my ribs.

A thousand times I started to sneeze and held it back with

an effort of will mighty enough to stop the world on its axis. Darkness, dust, the odor of antiquity and things long entombed, somewhere at hand a murderer with a gun.

Scared? I confess it without a blush. Only a fellow with carrot-hued hair, freckly-faced grin and a voice from Broadway would not know enough to be scared. I could have kicked his shins!

Eventually there was light. Gradually the darkness faded into a peculiar amber-colored twilight that revealed the tunnel as a corridor walled with ancient wooden panels and floored with dust-carpeted flags. At once it was a blessing and another danger. And where the devil was it coming from?

It was while I hunted the source of this illumination that I first discovered the mirrors. There was one set in the wall where the tunnel made its next twist. It caught my picture as I approached, sneaking; I thought it was a man stalking toward me and almost yelled.

Then I saw that this mirror was set in position to catch the light thrown from a glass farther down the tunnel. The glass shed light reflected from still another series of mirrors which seemed to be catching light from a shaft in the tunnel roof.

Farther on, the corridor was similarly lighted. Light from a shaft dropping from the hill's surface far above was tossed from mirror to mirror for the faint illumination of that underground trail.

Moonlight. I tell you, it was weird, startling and remarkable. A device invented by a genius who must have worked it out while Buddha sat in trances under *bo* trees. Another piece of 500 B.C. engineering, possible only to a country like Asia. Remember, the Chinese were making glass while Europe combed its hair by staring into a pool and America was learning the use of fire. How those mirrors got into Cambodia from China was something else again.

But there they were in the tunnel, and there were Johnny Ash and I. Again, there was the Dutchman with his cockney mate. Now we could plainly see in the mouse-gray dust blanketing the tunnel floor.

**JOHNNY ASH** hurried after them, chuckling; abruptly his chuckles stopped and he voiced a queer croak.

The tunnel had begun to zigzag like a puzzle box, and we stumbled across *it* at the second sharp turn. It lay directly under one of the light shafts, sprawled flat on its back, its crimson visage staring at the tiny points of moonlit sky visible far above. Scarlet threads leaked from its ugly leer. Its left temple had been bashed to a pulp by the handle of, say, a heavy automatic. It was, of course, the body of the little cockney mate!

A vicious curse escaped Johnny Ash.

"That Dutchman did this job. Wanted the treasure for himself alone. Do you see this, pal? Say. I'm going to get that louse an' get him good."

Johnny started to run. His blue eyes were diamonds in his face and his jaw came out a foot. Mad? I should say he was mad. The knuckles showed white on his fists as he pounded along the tunnel; and I raced after him with the fear of the Lord in my heart. He'd forgotten his fortune, now. He only wanted to get the brute who could strike down a man in cold blood.

The tunnel was getting lighter at every turn, and mirrors were everywhere. Suddenly we came to a turn where the underground corridor branched off into six other lanes. My companion raced straight ahead. And then we were sprinting through a regular rabbit-warren of intersecting hallways, twisting, turning, dodging that way and this, running us round and round.

At once we were lost in a wild confusion of interlacing paths. Mirrors at every angle in the walls added to the madness of the place. Have you seen those crazy-rooms in American amusement parks? You get into them and can't find a way out. That was the way with this subterranean *cul-de-sac;* and it didn't take me long to realize we were lost in a clever little Chinese trap. It might take us ten years to find the right path out of there.

Chance alone led my feet down the corridor leading to the cavern. There was a door visible at the corridor's end, and I flung it open with a prayer that it might lead us into the main tunnel, again.

The old wood casement moved with a hollow groan. Dust smoked under my hands and rust flaked from hinges fashioned before the days of Athens.

The red-head and I stumbled over the door sill together and never heard the old door slam behind us. Blind, we stood. Dazed. Stunned.

It was like plunging at one leap from night into day. Ali Baba admitted to the den of the Forty Thieves could not have been as astounded!

What a cavern that was! Fancy a room fifty feet broad and a hundred long, its ceiling thirty feet above the floor, and the whole made of glass. No opium smoker's dream could have conjured such a picture. The room was illuminated by a single shaft in the ceiling which dropped a pool of moonbeams that were scattered by a thousand mirrors.

That room was a madhouse of mirrors. Walled with mirrors. Mirrors set in the ceiling. Mirrors set in the floor. So that the cavern seemed to wander off into a thousand similar caves, and the occupant saw himself standing in a thousand different attitudes in as many different rooms.

Only one spot in that amazing, demoniac vault was not covered by a looking glass. The end of the room was piled high with lumpy leather bags. And that dying monk on the beach had not exaggerated. He had not. He had told of a fortune to rival the fanciest fortunes of the world's richest kings, and there it lay.

Gold!

It spilled from those time-rotted sacks in glittering cascades. It lay in gleaming mounds on the floor. It fell in spirals, coils and loops between the piled, decaying bags, shining as only gold can shine and catching and throwing moonbeams through the myriad fantasy-rooms pictured on the mirror-hung walls.

Gold dust, gold coin, gold amulets, gold tikals, gold bars and cubes and nuggets big as cherries. The treasure of a Cambodia dead before Angkor Vat. Lord above, what a fortune!

And the only spot in the room not covered by a mirror, I say, was a strip of sand that lay across the floor like a brown carpet stretched before that monstrous pyramid of riches. A strip of sand some thirteen feet wide, reaching from wall to wall and so on for miles into the mirrors.

Exactly in the center of this carpet of dull brown sand, his back toward us, his face toward the golden treasure, stood the giant Dutch skipper of the Houri. His automatic hung in the fist at his side. The handle of the automatic was bloodied.

## CHAPTER V

# HIDDEN DOOM!

**THE RED-HEAD AND** I couldn't have made a noise or stirred a muscle if we had been stabbed by a needle. There was only one sound in that amazing vault—the stertorous breathing of the Dutchman who stood glaring at those gold-stuffed leathern sacks. He hadn't heard our entry. He was feasting on that stupendous fortune; eating it with his eyes while the wind snored out of his lungs.

Then a Dutchman's curse slipped from his teeth; he flung out a lusting hand and snatched a bag to swing it on his shoulder. Ropes of muscle jutted on his bare arm and he swung sack to back with the ease of a stevedore picking up a loaf of bread.

That bag was heavy, too. He grunted under its weight, and a little trickle of yellow dust leaked from a broken seam in the leather.

Then he flung around and saw us!

Never in my life have I seen such an expression of bull fury come to the face of a human being. The man was a gargoyle standing there on that carpet of sand at the other end of the cave. Every nerve in his face contorted to make it a mask of rage.

His great, black-toothed mouth split in a horrendous grin and a savage oath rumbled out of his chest as his eyes went scarlet with venom. Sinews bulged on his tattooed forearm as it gestured to shift the weight of the sack on his shoulder.

The gun springing up from his belt made a dull flash, and its blunt muzzle spouted white flame as it fired. The quick shot clanged like the slam of an iron door in that underground cave. The result was a melodious smash that rang out like a stroke on a gong.

Do you know what happened? I knew it even as I jumped aside with a shriek and spilled in collision with Johnny Ash. That Dutch fiend hadn't shot at us. He had aimed at a reflection in a mirror! His flaming gun had smashed a panel of glass.

Right then I discovered an astounding thing. We ourselves had not actually seen the Dutchman. We had seen a mirrored reflection of the man and the carpet of sand and the bags of gold. To this day I do not know whether we were even in the same room with him or not. That amazing cave was nothing but a trick looking-glass room.

Can you imagine yourself trapped in a chamber walled with mirrors? You go to run and come up crashing against glass. You turn corners and find yourself face to face with your own reflection. In one corner you seemed to be in a long room. In another corner you were face to face with a mirror.

I could glimpse Johnny Ash's phantom shape dodging in a thousand reflections. I could see the Dutchman standing there with the sack on his back and the gun waving in his fist.

My brain whirled. My betrayed eyes went dizzy. I didn't know whether the enemy was behind me or in front of me. His gun spouted sharply and spots of glass showered into fragments with a harmonious smash—each separate mirror smashing with a different tone. But he was only shooting at our reflections.

Himself, he stood planted there on the sandy strip of floor. One—two—three he fired. The room sang with the echo. I dodged and sprawled and banged my face against glass screens. And then I saw something else. Something to bring another squawk out of my neck.

The Dutchman's feet were gone! Gone, I say. He didn't appear to notice it. He was wildly trying to sight with his gun; bewildered; cursing with rage. But his feet had disappeared in the sand.

Even as I watched—did I see him or a reflection in a mirror?—he sank to his knees. In half a moment he was down to the hips and screaming.

Then I understood what had happened to all those adventurers who had found the gold and vanished from the face of the earth. That sanded carpet was a crust over a well of quicksand. The weight of a man alone would not break through the crust. But the added weight of a heavy sack of gold would cause the holder's boots to break through; and he would be lost in the sucking toils.

Perhaps the cockney had guessed that trick, too. That was why he had carried away with him, on his first visit, only a palmful of coins.

**I SAW** the Dutchman drop his deadly burden and fight to free his legs.

Too late. The ponderous sack sank almost immediately. That sand must have been like gluey water.

Screaming wildly, the Dutch skipper struggled like a madman. His frenzied squirming drove him under to the armpits. I tell you, it was one horrible picture. He knew he was gone, and he wanted only to get the red-head and me. He shot the last three slugs from his automatic with desperate speed.

Panes of glass fell crashing. Powder-smoke clouded the air. The last three echoes clamored away like gong-notes.

The Dutchman's chest was under. The sand had him by the throat; choked quiet his terrible outcry as it closed over his mouth. His face vanished. Quietly the lethal sand rippled over his head.

One upraised hand clawed horridly at the air; went under as a knotted fist. And the deady brown carpet was undisturbed, again.

I heard Johnny Ash's voice howling behind me, and spun around to find him there in flesh and blood. Sweat was dropping from his chin; wiggling out of the red wig on his skull. His cheeks were the color of grass sprouting under a dead log, but his grin wasn't gone and his fingers were strong on my wrist.

I didn't know what he was saying, if anything, and I wanted only to get out of where I was. There were slivers of glass sprinkled around at my feet; brown blobs and patches where bullets had knocked six mirrors down from the wall; and I wanted to get away from the view of that empty brown carpet stretching before the piles of gold.

Luck played me an ace card. The barren patch of wall at my elbow was the only reality in that place of death and illusion, and I leaned a sick body against it. Promptly it fell outward. The mirror which had once been there had concealed the back of a door.

I went through the door at a bound, dragging the red-head after me. It closed gently; and we stood in the half-light of one of those many underground passages through which we had trailed. Somehow we began to run. I remember laughing with hysteria. And I remember Johnny Ash suddenly stopping me, and yelling:

"Say. We'll run around in these passages for years. Listen. You remember what that monk said for us to do after we found the gold? 'Do right,' he said. I got his idea now. Come on."

Chalk up one for that song-writing kid from Broadway. Of

course he'd hit the idea. Do right! That was the monk's way of telling us to take every turn to the right once we got out of that vault. We took every turn to the right.

Somewhere we jumped over the body of the cockney where he lay murdered, grim and grinning up at a light shaft. Then we were back in the main tunnel, sprinting for all we were worth, only anxious to get as far as possible from a mirror-tortured cave with its carpet of doom.

I had caught my second wind by the time we reached that portion of the tunnel where it was dark. Johnny Ash was clattering along at my heels, and we raced like Olympic relay men.

"SAY," I heard him yell, "can you smell it?"

I should say I could. Smoke! The dark was choked with smoke. Wood-smoke. Somewhere up ahead there was a fire. I recalled the red-head's pocket lighter placed at the tunnel's ancient door, and I squalled.

Now we really ran. Embers floated like fireflies about us and soon the smoke became a throttling rope around our necks. A nice little climax to end one lovely night's adventure in hell. That pocket lighter which was to guide us back to the world had set fire to the exit.

We rounded a corner, and dashed into a blazing funnel. The ancient wooden door of the tunnel was crumbling in varicolored flame and tongues of fire were lapping along the tunnel's paneled walls and ceiling with a joyous crackly noise.

The red-head and I tore through that last burning section like projectiles, I swear. No sprinting champions ever made a faster finish. We rushed through the merry bonfires, sprang through the fiery door and hurled ourselves into open air with sparks glowing in our clothes and embers singeing our hair.

And not a split minute-tick too soon, either, for a second after we lunged from that blaze-wrapped tunnel-mouth the shale cliffside fell with a tumultuous roar. Like the collapse of a fire-eaten section in a mine.

Those flame-ravaged walls fell in and the cliff tumbled down with a bawl. It spilled like an avalanche over the mouth of the Buddhist shrine. It poured down in a flood of sliding earth, shouting with that valiant rumble that only falling hills can make, heaving and bounding, hurling rocks and bowlders and pebbles and clods, raising a mighty bouquet of dust.

The shrine in the cliff was buried deep, lost under tons of earth. The porcelain image of Buddha's Blue Cat was shattered by winging rocks.

Johnny Ash and I, as though mummified, stood at a distance and watched the destruction. When it was done a streak of rose was glowing on the eastern horizon and the echoes were dying in the jungle, ripe with dawn.

The body of the Blue Cat was a mound of china fragments. But the head had been knocked off clean as a whistle by a flying rock.

Drawn by some unfathomable impulse, my companion and I tiptoed up to have a look at that crazy head. The pocket mirror was still jammed in its eye. Cracked down the middle, that mirror was, and with the glass turned skyward it caught a perfect picture of the four things hanging above in the aged banyan tree.

# EPILOGUE

BRADSHAW SPRAWLED BACK in his chair, reached a hand for the bottle, and tossed down the gin with a queer laugh.

"So the kid from Broadway didn't find his fortune after all," I remarked, for something to say.

The gaunt naturalist laughed, again. The orchestra in the hotel had launched into its final number, and was playing once more the popular song that had, somehow or other, started my friend on his incredible story. Now he sat chuckling, tapping time. Then he said:

"That's the story, old man. Johnny Ash and I made tracks

back to Lua Kapong. Remember the old warehouse on the outskirts? The tin shed where the Dutchman wrenched the confession out of the cockney? We had just about enough presence of mind to stop in there and pick up those three gold pieces the little mate had dropped. We gave two of 'em to the French hotel keeper, and that scorpion fixed us up with an outfit to trek overland with. When we got to Kampot on the coast we sold the other coin to a French collector, divided a hundred dollars between us, and hit for civilization. I went up to Bangkok, and I don't know where the red-head cleared for.

"I got to thinking, up in Bangkok; about that fortune buried under that hill back in Lua Kapong. Incidentally, I sent an outfit back to dig for it, and they dug for a whole year and couldn't locate anything but mud. They couldn't find the light shafts or the tunnel or anything. Later, a geologist told me the whole underside of that cliff and that hill must have been rotten with quicksand. The landslide had started a general undermining, and that damned cavern might be halfway to the middle of the earth. As for me, I wouldn't have gone back to that place in person for all the money in the world.

"So I hit for New York to forget about it. I landed in the States some months later than I had expected; and the first person I ran into was Johnny Ash. Listen! A Rolls-Royce cruised up to the curb where I was loitering. In front of the Astoria, it was. And who should step out from behind a swanky chauffeur but that red-head himself. I said, 'What the hell?' That kid looked like a million dollars, you understand. A cool million!

" 'Say,' I barked, 'did you go back and get that fortune out of there?' He just grinned, and said: 'Pal, come to this show tonight and see me afterward!' And handed me a theater ticket. I went to the show. He came out on the stage and warbled that song. The hit of the year. The Broadway smash.

" 'I'm cleaning up a fortune on it!' he chuckled to me afterward. 'Do you get it, pal? Remember! Say, I *knew* I'd find a fortune out there. Wrote this on the boat comin' home, and I'm makin' a fortune out of it.'

"Can you beat a guy like that? You bet I remembered. The first six notes of that song will haunt my dreams till I die and make 'em bad. Why, the six starting notes of his little ballad were the sounds of that Dutchman's bullets smashing those mirrors in the treasure cave. Sure. Weird notes. The echo of breaking mirrors. And the red-head remembered 'em an' wrote 'em into a million-dollar song. Wow and Lordy!"

Yes; when I came to think of it, those notes *did* sound like breaking mirrors. Modern jazz always wants something new. And what a song it was! Of course, the words put it over, too. The red-head had named it cleverly:

*"I'll See You in My Broken Looking-Glass!"*

# THE LITTLE GOLD
# DOVE OF GOJJAM

*In the unknown mountains of Abyssinia, the
savage Christian kingdom in Africa's black
heart, two naturalists venture on a mad quest*

**AFRICA LAY TO** starboard—a tenuous, blue-black line etched sharply below the moon. A warm night breeze, freighted with a fragrance queer and heady, drifted across the luminous water. The breeze and the low tropic stars and the land beyond were enough to make us forget our presence aboard this steamer forcing its way through the Gateway to the East. Bradshaw joined us where we stood enchanted at the ship's rail; but we did not know the naturalist was there until he spoke.

"There's an old Arab proverb," he chuckled, suddenly touching my arm, "that says this: Believe half of what you hear of Africa and nothing of what you see." He pointed over the rail with his pipe-stem. "I'm inclined to think that adage was written particularly for that bit of Africa lying yonder. The parcel of country just behind those coastwise hills. Know the land I mean? I'm speaking of Abyssinia."

He fixed the shoreline with a dreamy gaze while his lean fingers stoked his pipe with that tobacco he insisted on smoking. I caught a hint of cognac as he breathed, and I knew his tone. There would be a story forthcoming if the young British consular agent standing with me didn't say something fatuous and shut the naturalist up. The young consular agent was "going out" for the first time. He hadn't been down this Red Sea before, and he didn't know the naturalist as I did.

"Abyssinia!" I urged. And in all truth the name of that little-explored kingdom had trapped my interest. "I say, Bradshaw—

never knew you'd traveled in there. You've poked into every other God-forgotten spot on the globe, but you never mentioned Abyssinia before."

"It's the weirdest country in all the world!" He blew a ribbon of white smoke, and paused to watch it unfold. "Strangest land going, and least known. There it lies, landlocked behind those mountains; fenced in by Italian Eritrea and French Somaliland. Dinky railroad running from the French chunk of coast to her capital is her only modern touch. Old? The rulers of that black Ethiopian kingdom date back in unbroken line to the Queen of Sheba. And the country hasn't changed its ways since Bible times. No gentle kingdom, either. Italy tried to grab it off in 1896 and the Abyssinians smashed the force from Rome into a million pieces. Foreigners keep out of there. And if they don't, they should."

He turned on me with an abrupt gesture. "I *was* in there a few years ago. I say! Haven't I ever told you about the little gold dove of Gojjam? No? Well, I don't tell the story very often. Too few people would believe. They haven't seen Abyssinia. It's the strangest land in the world, I tell you, and this story is stranger yet. I wouldn't tell it now, if the moon wasn't up...."

But the moon was up. So he balanced against the rail and worked his pipe and began:

**TUPPER** was your typical Englishman. He had light hair, decent blue eyes, a short nose and a businesslike jaw. Believed in tea, tweeds, the king and God. If his father hadn't been a rector in some polite London parish, this thing might never have happened. But John Tupper had been brought up on theology from Genesis to Revelation, and I guess he'd had a trifle too much of it.

He was religious enough, you understand, but he was a little fed up on the subject, time he reached twenty-five; so instead of following his father's expectations and going out as a missionary, he got drunk one day and landed a job as a naturalist.

The Paris outfit took him on; and first thing I knew, a young

*That black was fighting like sevin devils.*

Britisher by the name of John Tupper walked down the gang-plank at Jibouti to shake me by the hand.

He had been sent down to go with me as my assistant on a trek into the heart of Abyssinia.

I sized him up as a good lad; and we started out. We were to railroad from Jibouti into Abyssinia to Addis Abbaba, the capital. From there we were to trek into the hinterland mountains after specimens. Rare specimens. And those Abyssinian mountains are the places to find rare specimens, don't forget it.

Maybe you've heard of those hills. The ancient geographers called them the Mountains of the Moon, and said you could find unicorns and werewolves and dragons in there by the carload. I didn't doubt it at all when we got into those hills. I've seen some lonely corners of the unknown in my day, but never a region as desolate as that. Here was the place where the ghosts of the universe gathered for their family reunions. The jumping-off place of the world. The north and south polar regions are roaring Times Squares compared to those Mountains of the Moon.

Now the *Jardin des Plantes* in Paris was hiring our time and energy. Wanted us to bring back a few clog-faced baboons, a colobus monkey, couple of cheetahs and koodoo antelopes, an ant-eater, one of those rare gazelles known as a nyala, and the rarest specimen of all, a certain yellow dove. And those exacting directors of the *Jardin* wanted something else. They wanted me to find some trace of Camille Caillard.

That yellow-winged dove was going to be hard to find; but if I knew anything about it, a trace of Camille Caillard was going to be harder to locate than a dodo. Perhaps you remember reading about Caillard in the papers. Caillard was that collector who brought back from Nepal the first armored rhinoceros ever seen. The world's greatest genius as a naturalist.

The *Jardin* had sent him into Abyssinia in those dangerous days before the Italian-Ethiopian War, and he had never come out. For two years the *Jardin* thought nothing of it. Caillard was a queer one, I say. Genius. He'd given up a wealthy business as one of Avignon's leading goldsmiths to indulge his passion for collecting. He would rave about a nice exhibit of taxidermy and he was in his seventh heaven when surrounded by unusual specimens. He was just the man to vanish into the unknown and turn up from nowhere after months of silence.

But after he'd been gone three years in Abyssinia, the zoological gardens began to worry. They sent a French emissary. He trailed Caillard to the Mountains of the Moon, then lost the track. Fifteen years had now elapsed. I was to pick up the trail if I could, as a sort of side-issue.

Well, young Tupper and I started our *safari* for the mountains without mishap. We had a good *safari*. Our boys were a wild-looking lot, wrapped in their white *chammas*, carrying shields and spears. Our guide was an Abyssinian noble, black as ink, gorgeously robed. We looked like a caravan procession out of the Middle Ages as we wound down the trail, and the ancient castles we'd occasionally pass helped out the picture.

Things went well. The fourth day out we had captured most

of our prizes. We had our ant-eater, cheetahs, baboons, monkey and koodoo antelopes. All we lacked was the rare nyala and the yellow dove and any trace of Camille Caillard.

**WHEN** we reached the foothills of those Mountains of the Moon, I knew Caillard was dead and gone. We had ridden into that part of the mountains where the Blue Nile rises, known as Gojjam. A wild land of arid hills, barren watercourses, steep escarpments, hot ragged cliffs and crags.

No spark of civilization had ever floated down the blazing sky that blistered the landscape. Jackals and hyenas roved the stony slopes and starved. Now and then we'd meet a tar-black, devil-looking horseman who'd wave a poisoned lance at us and ride off down the cliffs like a goat and make us mighty glad of the Webley pistols in our belts.

"There are ten thousand ways to die in these hills," I told Tupper. "Lions and sunstrokes and bandits and starvation. It would be mighty hard to track a man gone two days in this *cul-de-sac* of ravines; and Caillard has been gone fifteen years. Our guide promises me the man is dead. Even his bones are gone by now. We'll forget him and try to get hold of a nyala and that infernally rare dove."

We'd been riding down the rim of a cliff that was like an oven-lid in the blazing morning sun, and Tupper was tinkering with his binoculars. Just as I spoke he jumped in his saddle and got me by the arm.

"There's your nyala now," he barked. Sure enough. He'd spotted the beast bounding down the valley below. And off we went, helter-skelter.

I don't know how it happened. I guess Tupper and I rode the fastest ponies of the lot; and we had to speed like the devil if we wanted to get our hands on that gazelle. Our Abyssinian guide pounded along behind us, but we outdistanced him in no time. That nyala gazelle was covering ground like a ghost running before daylight, and we spurred our horses to the utmost.

Our prize fled up one ravine and down another, bounced along a crooked cañon and into a maze of arroyos, and, like the tinkling fools we were, Tupper and I raced after.

I think it was the hollow echo of the hoofbeats that finally brought me up with a jerk. I got a nice little shock when I realized our guide had dropped out of the picture, and I yelled to Tupper, telling him to stop. He'd lost sight of his confounded nyala, anyway, and he reined in with a grin.

"Nothing to grin about," I told him sourly, fanning with my helmet. "We left our guide somewhere behind, and we'd better find him quick. We'd be needles in a haystack if we ever got lost in these mountains."

Tupper chuckled and scrubbed at a sunburned nose. "I say, Bradshaw—lost? Lost in Abyssinia! What a blooming exciting adventure that would be. You could write a book about it, what?"

"You could write a murder yarn if you pull any more smart remarks like that," I rasped. "Nice adventure, eh? Let me tell you, the man who's lost his way in these hills is out of luck. Why, half of these mountains are unexplored, unmapped. You saw those lions roaming around yesterday, and those black tribesmen who came to camp. Nothing to joke with. We'll fire a few shots right now to bring that guide along."

Tupper was game enough and had proved a clever rifle-shot and a companionable assistant, but he lacked experience. He'd never trailed into hinterland mountains before, and he took a grin on a native's face to mean friendship. One of those stanch Britons who believed the Union Jack would shadow him into any corner of the world.

I knew something else. It's a scary business, dropping over the edge of the world into some unknown African range. Those Abyssinians might have been converted Christians, but they looked to me like lads who'd cut your throat to get your sun helmet.

So I fired my rifle to bring the guide, and the echoing shots brought nothing but a bevy of buzzards. I didn't like the looks of it. I turned my horse and made for the trail back.

In five minutes I knew I couldn't find the trail back. Then we rode. We topped ridges and played lookout. We fired signal-shots. We galloped up one hill and down another. Then we stood on a cliff buttress for an hour, firing at intervals. The echoes died away in the cañon below. The sun reached its zenith and destroyed every vestige of shade and the last of my good humor. And not a trace of our *safari* could be seen. We were lost.

**IF YOU** think I didn't do some first-class cussing you're wrong. I cussed the broiling sun, the silence, the guide for being deaf. I could have kicked myself purple for catapulting after that gazelle. Even Tupper was getting uneasy. We rode down the valley; and every mile the mountains got bigger and we got smaller and the silence thick as cotton.

The sun started to climb down out of the sky and the mountains turned from scarlet to dull red. Lonely? It was so lonely you found yourself talking in whispers and darting nervous glances over your shoulder. Every step our mounts took seemed to trap them deeper in that puzzle of crags and cañons.

No living thing seemed to inhabit that valley. Even the jackals weren't to be seen. The silence poured from the sky and up out of the rocks, and we couldn't seem to break it by firing our rifles. Those gun-shots sounded like twigs snapping against the vast escarpments of stone. The cliffs towered like castles against the metal sky, and the winds that played between them were gusts of a smelter furnace.

"This is hell," Tupper suggested, waving his gun. "I'll be fried to a cinder by the sun in another hour. And a human voice would sound mighty good to me, too, I'll—"

A human voice! The words weren't out of his mouth when we heard the scream. What a scream! It split through that mountain quiet as a gunshot never could, and it sat us stiff in saddle with the hair prickling on our necks. Again the ghastly cry bit into the silence and echoed soprano among the crags. It seemed to come from just beyond a steep ridge; it conveyed the very essence of terror; and it made the sweat boil out on my face. A banshee wail if I ever heard one.

Tupper forced the words from a mouth full of dough, "Good God, what was that?"

I answered by spurring up the ridge.

**WHAT** we saw drove the breath from our lungs, I can tell you that. The slope tilted down to a little bowl-like valley, and in this valley a big black man and an enormous tawny lion were fighting.

It was the black man who was letting out those awful screams, and no wonder. The lion had its teeth in the man's left shoulder, its fore paws on his chest, its hind feet madly trying to claw the black's middle. From the looks of things the lion had just made its spring; by a miracle it had missed its mark at the victim's throat. And, armed with a knife only, that black was fighting like seven devils. Locked together in a death clutch, man and beast rolled on a mat of blood, scattering a vermilion shower.

I shot from the saddle, which was lucky, for the black man was almost gone. The lion went limp, and the shrieking native dragged free his mangled body and lay naked and bleeding on the stones. Tupper and I got to his side in a big hurry, and the minute I got a real look at him I knew he was done for.

We couldn't do anything but drag him into the shade of a giant bowlder; and Tupper touched a water-bottle to his writhing lips. And then we got a surprise. That Abyssinian rolled his eyes up at us and shoved the word out of his grinding teeth. "Thanks!"

"You speak English!" I said in astonishment.

"Yes." He panted and moved his head.

"Where did you come from," I marveled.

He juggled his bloodied hand. "Many years ago—me—went America. New York. Shine shoes. Get money. Come back. Fight for King Menelik. Me—Abyssinian. Name Mefwik. You kill lion—save—my life—"

There he lay in the cheerless, hot shade of that bowlder deep in that lost valley of the Abyssinian hinterland mountains, a dying black native, thanking us for saving his life and speaking the King's English. It got me by the throat, I can tell you. Made me want to pinch thyself to see if I was real.

I don't think Tupper was as astounded. He didn't know how far off the beaten track we were. And that black had spoken of New York! Shining shoes! A Negro shine-boy blacking boots in the lobby of some skyscraper on Broadway. No, not a Negro. The Abyssinians are black Caucasians. But they don't speak English and thank you for saving their lives. Only we hadn't saved this fellow's life, either. He started to cough and blood bubbles came to his lips.

"He's dying," Tupper muttered; and the native suddenly grinned: "Yes."

I poured some more water through his teeth, and he got up on one elbow. "That lion—he follow me all morning. I think I leave him behind. But he catch. You save me from him. You my friends. You I reward."

I wanted to question him before he went completely out of his head. "How'd you get in this valley?" I asked. "You and that lion are the first living things we've seen for miles. Where are we? Can you tell us where lies the main trail?"

His eyes rolled like white moons and the crimson grin widened on his face. "I alone. This a forbidden valley. No man dare come here. God will punish. See. He has punished me. I die. No man should come to this valley. No. But I did not believe and I come. Now I die."

His tone of voice brought the damp out on my face. Tupper was impressed, too. He leaned over the wretched creature. "I say now. Why? Why should no one come into these hills?"

The teeth clacked in the black's jaw. "They sacred. This valley sacred. Look. Many years ago, many years before Solomon—

before the Lion of Judah—long, long back there was the flood. The flood! It was here." He fell back with a groan. "You listen? Then I tell you. Listen well."

And into our astonished ears, that dying Abyssinian poured out the story of the flood. *The* flood, you understand. In faltering, fragmentary sentences he strangled out that story known to every infant in Sunday school; while Tupper and I listened and didn't believe our hearing. The story from Genesis. The story of Noah and the Ark!

**CAN YOU** imagine how preposterous the whole thing was? That poor black devil was dying—dying from the claws of the lion that lay down the slope with my bullet in its skull and the flies already feeding on its hide—and that Abyssinian was spending his last efforts to tell us the story of Noah's Ark.

I wasn't so surprised to hear an Abyssinian recite a Bible story. Around 300 A.D. Christianity was carried into Ethiopia by the Phœnician, Frumentius. About the time of Pedro da Covilham, a lot of Portuguese monks went in there and firmly established the religion. The Abyssinians are Coptic Christians, and devout. Many of those tribesmen know the Good Book better than present-day New Yorkers.

But this black man's method of telling and his version of the story was what got under my skin. He described the flood and the Ark and Noah in vivid detail. And he added a piece I'd never heard before.

"And two of every animal," he panted on, "was put in the great Ark. Yes. And then Noah took his gold. Much gold. More gold than any king would have. Yes. Noah put his gold in the Ark, too."

The eyes bulged in his graying face as he told us about Noah storing his treasure in the Ark. His tongue flickered over his lips as he told us about that gold, and you would have thought he was seeing it.

"Much—much gold. In the Ark. And then the rain came. Noah, he sail away. Where do he sail? The Ark float over these mountains. The water go away. The Ark—it is in these mountains. In a little lake. It is there. There—"

His breath gave out with a gurgle, and we gave him a little more of our precious water, and he almost sat up.

"That—that my story. Every Abyssinian know it. They know Noah and the Ark—full of animals and gold—sail over these mountains—and stop here. That why these valleys are sacred. Yes. No man should come here. When I am a boy the priest of the Coptic shrine at Lalibela, he tell me the story. I do not believe. I go to America. When I hear the story in that great country—I believe. America is wise. It, also, tells of Noah and the Ark. So I believe—and come back here. I come back," he groaned, "to *see* this Ark. To find it. I come back to—steal the gold!"

His face was contorted with pain as he said that, and he flopped on his side.

"The poor devil is making a confession," I whispered to Tupper. "A dying confession. He thinks Heaven is punishing him for a heresy. He probably believes the Lord sent that lion to slay him—"

"The Lord kill me for doing wrong!" he exclaimed, grabbing at my arm. "I die. But wait. I tell you. This story of Noah—it true. The Ark—it here! Along about five mile. There you see a lake. The Ark is in that lake! *I saw the Ark!*" His eyes were wide and his fingers bit into my arm, "The Ark—I saw. *I saw Noah! The animals! The gold!*"

He yelled out those words, and suddenly the flesh crawled along my spine. He had seen the Ark and Noah and a hoard of gold. Whew! It was raving nonsense, of course. I'd heard legends of men finding traces of the Ark. I knew, too, that the Abyssinians believed that certain of the saints lived on forever, leading recluse lives where human mortals couldn't find them, fasting and praying in hermit caves and dying only on that day when Gabriel's horn should depopulate the earth.

But here was a man who claimed he had seen one. Noah. And his Ark and treasures.

There was something in his voice that made his words sound true. I couldn't believe his story, and I couldn't disbelieve it.

He had stolen into these forbidden hills to see the Ark and he had seen it! I shot a look at Tupper. Beads of sweat were glittering on the Englishman's forehead. He shot a strange look at me. Then he bent over the dying black man.

"Where?" His voice was low and harsh and throaty. "I say, where is this Ark that you saw?"

"I tell you." The Abyssinian whispered and a thread of blood leaked from his teeth. "Five—maybe ten mile. Up this valley. The river start there. You see trees. A big lake. The Ark and Noah—and the treasure—on that lake—"

His white eyes stared and a ghastly pallor suffused his dark cheeks. A sudden spasm convulsed his mangled frame, and his worries were over.

I don't know how long Tupper and I squatted there like sticks, glaring at that poor dead devil. I know the sun was westering and shadows had crept up the slope when Tupper finally spoke. He pivoted on his heels and his eyes were queer in his face as he reached out and got me by the sleeve.

"Bradshaw!" he rasped. "I say, Bradshaw. I believe him. Men don't lie with their dying breath. This fellow spoke the truth. So come along. I want to see this lake he told of. I—I want to see the Ark!"

Lord forgive me, I wanted to see it, too!

**WELL,** it all had happened so suddenly it sounds like madness. The native and the lion had appeared as if by magic; I'd shot the lion in half a wink; and the native had rewarded us with his amazing story in less time than it takes to tell. But that was Abyssinia and things are different in Abyssinia, you bet you are!

To understand why Tupper and I started down that valley believing we'd find something as almighty ridiculous as Noah's

Ark, you'd have to see those vast and vacant cliffs towering up to touch the sky and listen in on that monstrous silence.

You know the queer feeling it gives you to stare up the side of a tall building or look down into a deep gorge with a tiny river at its bottom. That's the way I felt in those lost mountains of the Gojjam region. It was just the place for a dying native to spin a yarn of pure nonsense and make it sound rational. And it was just the yarn to make two fools forget they were lost.

Then it occurred to me we weren't lost, at that. The reason our guide hadn't turned up was because the valley was sacred and forbidden. No doubt if we rode straight on for a few hours we'd ride out of the forbidden area and locate our Abyssinians again. However, I wasn't of the mind to rationalize. And Tupper had an expression on his face queer as madness.

"Think of it," he kept gasping. "Noah's Ark—here! And Noah!"

"Noah!" I snapped. "Say, don't let your reason run away from you altogether. No doubt that native saw something. Maybe he saw the actual ruins of the Ark where it was stranded in one of these inland lakes. But he never saw those animals or Noah, himself. You don't mean to tell me you believe that part of the crazy yarn!"

Tupper didn't reply. He just jabbed spurs into his horse. I never saw an Englishman so robbed of his traditional British calm. A cord was standing out on his jaw and a little trickle of sweat wiggled down the side of his nose. To see him so upset sort of reminded me I was acting like an idiot.

"This is blithering nonsense," I told myself; but I chased him up the shadowing trail just the same.

Meantime the afternoon was waning. If there was anything to see I wanted to see it before darkness set in. I spurred, too. The echo of beating hoofs conjured a legion of invisible horsemen riding down the cliffs that fenced the valley in. The sun was a crimson globe hung low in a sky of burned umber. Grotesque shadows carpeted our stony trail; and sure enough, we hadn't gone a mile farther before evidences of vegetation substantiated the native's story of a forest and a land-locked lake where a river might rise.

Then Tupper rounded a sharp headland that jutted out of the valley's cliff-fence, and held up a hand with a yell.

"Look! Trees!" He sat his saddle, pointing; and I was able to stare up a long pebbly slope patrolled at the top by a line of stalwart eucalyptus which stood like graven etchings against the sky. Behind the trees a gibbous cloud-bank rested like a blossoming white mushroom; and I knew there must be a lake lying under that horizon.

It was a surprise, I tell you. The native had promised us those trees would be there, but it was like coming across a New England farm sprouting green in the middle of the Sahara.

Well, we raced up the slope as fast as our tired mounts could go, but it had altered from maroon to blue in coloring by the time we gained its top, and the sun had sunk in sky-sea painted in pink.

I wish I could describe the view we found when we stood in the shadow of those tall eucalyptus trees at ridge-top. The whole thing was like a mirage. The valley below must have been the crater of a monstrous volcano blown open when the world was young. Miles away, on the other rim of the crater, one caught a hazy glimpse of a divide down which a river could have wandered westward to the back of beyond.

Now the divide made a cup for the sunset, and the peaks on either side were nesting places for low clusters of cloud. The inner walls of this crater were massed with brilliant green, blanketed with jungly forest. And like a mirror at the crater's bottom, flat and glistening, spread the enameled waters of the mountain lake.

**NO TIME** to stop and stare. Already the pink was fading from that patch of sunset sky. The evening clouds were fattening.

From the region of cliffs we had left behind, a yellow round moon was rising.

Wordless, Tupper and I started down through the trees, seeking a path to the bottom. A mile or so down we found one. Rank, weed-grown, it meandered like a creek through the thickening forest. Darkness set in, and damp. We pushed along, depending on the faint luminescence of the rising moon.

Now and then we could glimpse patches of the lake below, or see the rim of the crater across the broad valley. Clouds were gathering there in dead earnest, and there was a hint of rain. We pushed our lathering horses faster. We wanted to get down to the shore of that lake.

When we did, Tupper was still leading. Through the wedge of trees we caught a view of dark water and a spread of beach. I remember a squad of herons that started up from the water and flapped away, hooting mournfully. Small animals under foot, too. What a sportsman's paradise that place would have been! But I wasn't thinking of that. I could only think of that lake and what we might see when we stood on its shore.

Impossible that we should have seen anything, of course, for the lake was miles long. Why it should have been anywhere near the point where we should come out on the beach was nothing but madman's luck.

Tupper rode through a sandalwood grove and out under a gnarled baobab tree, and I heard him utter an astonished yell. I rode out behind him. Our horses stood on a little fan of shore, bright under the moon-washed sky. The green of the jungly forest reared behind us. Dark water scribbled with the gold of moonbeams lay before. Tupper was glaring at a shadow resting on the ripples perhaps a mile offshore. The eyes were starting from his head, and his mouth labored to frame the words.

"*The Ark!*"

**NOAH'S ARK!** I give you my word, I almost flopped from my saddle in astonishment. For there was that improbable craft floating before my very eyes; and if it wasn't the Ark of Noah,

I'd like to have known, right then, what it was. You know those little wooden Noah's Arks they sell in toy stores? Here was one of them, enlarged ten million times, drifting in those backwaters of that lost Abyssinian lake.

No ship was ever built in such a way. Here was a huge, floating barn with blunt prow and stern and high roof—an enormous wooden barge grotesque with funny projecting balconies and odd tiers of windows. And even from a distance we could see the affair was old.

Old? It looked as ancient as the sky. Mats of fungi clung to that awkward hull. Vines and patches of moss looped from the edge of the sagging roof. A queer tangle of weeds appeared to hang on its landward side to give it a starboard list. Drifting full in the moonlight, the thing was a phantom, gray and ghostly—a wraith escaped from the earliest pages of the Old Testament. I tell you, it gave me a turn.

How we stared! And then Tupper was in the lake; I after him. We swam. Starved, lost, tired we were, but we never remembered it. The shock of the plunge in cold water never brought sense to our brains, either. We swam toward that floating relic like a relay team.

Afterward I looked this up in the Bible and memorized the details. According to the Good Book, the Lord told Noah to make himself an ark three hundred cubits long, fifty wide and thirty high. The divine voice told Noah to build the ark in three stories and fix a door in the roof. Let me tell you, this barge in that Abyssinian lake was built tallying to directions. When we neared the thing and I distinguished a gangway lowered down the side of the hull, leading from water's edge to a broad doorway in the sloping roof, I could have drowned in abject astonishment.

A pale mist had started to smoke up from the lake surface. Shot through with shafts of moonbeams, the vapor wreathed gently about the black hull and made it more hoary and weird than ever.

Tupper carried himself to the craft with strong overhand strokes; swung, dripping, on to the gangway; beckoned me to follow. I won't forget the way my stomach knotted when I clambered up beside him. The wooden handles of that gangway were greasy with damp must. Under foot the wood was slippery, covered with moss. Great barnacles decorated the hull at water's edge, and the planks looked waterlogged and rotten.

The old hulk was drifting slowly, and the moving water whispered, lapping at the rotted wood. The whole affair was so dank and eerie I'd have been contented to leave her, then, and swim away. Not so Tupper. He was up the gangway without a word. Grinning fatuously, I trailed him. Fancy swinging up the gangway of Noah's Ark! Creepy's the word. Like poking your nose into an Egyptian tomb or leaning against the Sphinx.

Just as we gained the gaping door in the roof the moon burrowed into a haze of smoky cloud and the moonlight turned green. It was then I noticed the sullen phalanx of thunderheads that had swiftly crowded the rest of the sky. No breeze riffled the water of the lake below. The air was taut, apprehensive. Wringing water off my wrists, I glared at Tupper, who stood staring into that amazing door.

"**LOOK** here, Tupper," I said—and my voice seemed to break a quiet that had been solid for a million years. "Look here! We're forgetting our reason. We better get off this hulk in a hurry. There's a storm coming up. I've been in storms on these African lakes before. They're tornadoes."

The Englishman hadn't spoken ten words since we'd heard that native's yarn back among the crags, and he did not speak now. Maybe you wouldn't have talked, yourself, if you'd been standing in the main hatchway of Noah's Ark. Tupper, remember, was young; and he'd never before been out of England, where things work according to rule.

The moonlight was green on his wet cheeks, and he had an expression on his face I never want to see anywhere again. I mean, there was no expression. Only his eyes were bright points of metal behind a dripping tangle of hair, and the breath kept sighing from his lips.

Without a word he stepped into that dank hatchway. Of course I was hard on his heels. A dead breeze smote us in the face as we crossed the doorsill, and a bat or something equally musty flickered over our heads. The phantasmal light of the thin-veiled moon dropped through narrow windows and revealed a barren passageway that breathed a scent of age.

I didn't want to walk down that passageway, but my companion stepped down it in a minute. Why, the whole thing was like the top floor of an abandoned hotel. A hundred empty rooms and odd-shaped compartments opened on the passage, and a hundred thousand rats scurried in retreat ahead of us.

"For God's sake be careful!" I warned, fearing our feet might crash through the rotten flooring any minute.

Tupper didn't hear. He'd found an open trap at the end of the passage, and I saw him disappear down a ladder. I clambered down after him, and found myself in a lofty, barn-wide room piled deep with bags and bales of stale grass. When I saw the grass I got a scare. Certainly some one had put it there!

Tupper glared at it, too, and started across the room toward a row of doors leading aft. He took four steps, and caught his foot on something and stumbled. When he gained his feet, I reached him, and found him gazing down at a huge brass ring fastened to the floor. Another trap door. Reaching down, he tugged on the ring, and the door lifted open. Right then I won the prize shock of my whole life!

**ANIMALS!** There must have been a hundred animals down in that dim, cavernous hold. Baboons, horses, cheetahs, antelopes, cats, lions, a giraffe. That broad, gloomy hold into which we glared was literally filled with an amazing congregation of beasts crowded together in the shadowy gloom—a gloom that smelled like the summed-up odor of ten thousand zoos.

Will you believe it when I say there were *two* of each species? Will you believe when I say those animals were standing tame, motionless? That astonishing menagerie! Here was a leopard poised beside a gazelle; a wild pig crouching at the feet of a pygmy hippo. Shadows massed in the dusk. Wow! I hung my face over the edge of that trap, looking down, and almost fell through.

For the sight of those animals may have been astounding, but the vision of the old man down there was utterly, monstrously unbelievable.

A steep ladder of narrow steps dropped from the trap where Tupper and I were hanging paralyzed with the wonder of it; and at the foot of these steps the old man sat. He sat hunched over a table, squinting at a tiny framework of bone on which his twig-like hands were working.

A bowl of tallow burned smokily at his elbow, the wavering flame-light casting an amber halo about his bent head. A snowy mane of hair flowed down his bowed shoulders, and his beard was a white waterfall that got in the way of his fingers as they tinkered. A loose white robe shrouded his withered frame. The aureole of light on his face found it a mask of parchment.

The mob of animals massed behind him seemed to watch him at work. As Tupper and I stared—too astonished for words—the pair of lions (lion and lioness, by Heaven!) disengaged themselves from the shadowy group and padded noiselessly about the ancient one's work-table. Tame? Tame as cats in a grocery.

The lioness rubbed against the old man's legs; the lion roamed around the table. The old man reached out to absently pat the beast's muzzle.

Save my soul, if those animals hadn't moved I'd have believed the entire thing a mesmeric delusion. Those motionless beasts standing in the gloom were so unreal, and the old, old man was so convincingly a dream. But the two lions did more than move. The lioness began to lash the tip of her tail. The lion growled. My ears couldn't have been fooled. And suddenly that lion swung its majestic head, stared up the ladder down which *we* glared, saw us with eyes like points of phosphorus, and roared! A mighty thunderclap of sound.

The vibrations of that terrific, silence-shattering bellow echoed like an explosion; seemed to start the deck a-tilting under us. The old man bounced up from his seat as if he'd been kicked. The lioness repeated her mate's roar. Lion, lioness and old man turned their eyes up the ladder and saw me.

I think the old man let out a yell. I know I did. God knows I'd wanted to yell for a long time. At least the silence was scattered away.

Tupper shouted something about Noah; and then the lions were pawing at the foot of the ladder, tails whipping, and the old, old whitebeard had a knife in his hand and fury in his eye.

If you don't believe lions can climb steps, you're crazy. The pair of them started topside with a spring. The old man came scrambling behind them, whiskers blowing, steamy gasps escaping from his open mouth. The murderous stiletto in his hand gleamed like a heated wire in the dimness. His eyes were livid coals.

You can bet Tupper and I danced away from the edge of that hatch. We didn't have time to shut the trap. We started back with a jump, came up against the bales of straw, wheeled like caged beasts in the dark, stumbled, ran.

There had been the glint of homicide in old man Noah's eyes. Those trained lions of his had looked mighty famished.

Two things more I noticed in that sudden wild burst of activity. I noted I was the world's champion damned fool for leaving my guns back on shore with the horses. I noticed that this dream-barge which I had invaded was suddenly rocking like a ship in mid-ocean. The deck reeled, tilting like a drunken sailor.

Tupper and I floundered frantically. Somewhere thunder was crashing. It sounded as if the sky had fallen, collapsed with a bang on the roof of that wallowing barn. A burst of rain hammered the creaking hull. A blinding half-second of lightning dissolved the darkness, revealed a row of windows gushing wet wind—and showed the head of the lioness poking up out of the hatch.

**WE BOLTED.** We fled among the bales of straw, seeking doors. We could hear the lions galloping after us; the old man uttering squeaky shouts. The dark was treacherous, the deck under foot a tilting trick. Once—several years after—I saw a movie comedy in which an escaped lion chased a pair of terrified comics through a maze of rooms. I guess our race was similar.

Tupper banged into a door, and we went through it fast. Down a weird passageway. Through another door. That nightmare of Noah and his pets followed fast. We didn't know our way. They knew theirs.

Outside it was storming. Thunder was falling down the heavens, crashing like smashing drums of glass. Lightning blazed. Now we'd be rushing through blank night. Then there'd be a second of glaring day. And every time we'd turn a corner we could glimpse our pursuers sweeping around the turn behind us: the galloping lions, the old man floating along in his white robe and brandishing his needle-like knife.

I tell you the thing was too fantastic for credence. That old Ark bowling through a storm. An Englishman and a Yankee sprinting around a dark puzzle chased by a legend and his trained pets. Twisting this way, dodging that, Tupper led the race. Somewhere we found a long alleyway, ran for all we were worth. A burst of lightning revealed two open windows at its end and a patch of black, boiling sky.

"The windows!" I screamed at Tupper. "Big enough for us to jump through. Come on!"

We were beside the ports in a second, black rain whipping at our heads. The sky outside split open, stabbed through and through with jagged bolts of white flame. The clouds boomed. I caught an eye-flicker picture of the lake below—a heaving, tumbling surf. Good Lord! the water was almost up to those ports. Spray smote my face. The waves climbed high. The barge rolled dangerously, groaned, shuddered, creaked.

"Quick!" I shrieked, grabbing at Tupper. "We must jump!"

The lightning played again. The vivid glow lit up that Englishman's face. What do you think? The man was laughing!

"Jump if you want to!" he howled. "You could have jumped when we were running aft—we passed twenty windows. But I'm staying."

"You're staying?" I squalled at him.

He laughed shrilly. "You bet I am! Those lions won't catch me. Noah won't either. I'm staying. *I'm going to find the gold!*"

"You fool!" I shrieked. "Find gold? Fool! You'll be caught in two jumps. Look—they're coming up the passage now. Jump!'

I snatched his wrist. He struggled. I could hear him laughing. I shoved him against the lurching sill of the port.

"I'm staying!" he screamed. "Go yourself!"

His fist drove into the side of my jaw and I flopped through the window into storming water. The waves whirled me head over heels. I was under. I was up. I swam, fighting through whitecaps. Through a blind and howling blackness I swam. Finally my feet touched bottom. A comber doubled me into a granny's knot, and flung me onto dry land. Land, anyway, however wet.

I lay on my back and the rain pelted my face. Finally the pelting became a gentle tapping. Exhausted, mentally dead, I must have slept. Thunder and tossing water muttered; were forgotten.

YOU KNOW how a violent storm will quickly attack a small lake and as quickly die out. When I dropped into sleep the rain had ceased. I woke with hot sunshine in my eyes. Steam was rising from my muddied clothes. I lay on a little fan of white beach backed by dripping, grass-green foliage.

With a hasty rush of memory, I leaped to my feet. Yes, there was the lake, cerulean under cloudless morning skies, rippling gently, burnished by the beams of the rising sun. I stared. The water was at peace. Distant across the water, the opposite shore was a sweep of emerald.

A clump of palms cut off the view where the beach on which I stood curved westward. Small parrots flitted among the fronds. Bugle-birds sang. A stork waddled up the shallows, sighted me, and flapped away. And I stared. I stared at the lake. Offshore about a mile, a brown smear on the surface marked a patch of roily water. A scatter of black spars drifted there. The rest of the Ark was gone!

Finally I gave up staring and forced my feet to plod up the sand. I felt pretty sick, too. I felt pretty lonely and ill. I ambled down the shore, and the sweat was prickling out on my face, and it was then I stumbled across the nyala gazelle. A nyala! The mockery of it. Undoubtedly it had been one of the Ark's menagerie, drowned and tossed landward by the storm. There it lay, legs stretched stiff, neck arched, head back. I wasn't interested in rare specimens at that moment. Dully I gazed at the dead beast. I could only remember my vanished companion, and Noah, and—Suddenly I was down on my knees glaring at that nyala gazelle. That nyala....

But I didn't get a chance to find out. I heard a sound. Bootheels crunching on sand. I looked up. And saw Tupper!

He wandered out of the grove of palms that screened the curve of beach farther westward. Wandered, I say. He came toward me at a shambling pace, but he didn't see me. His clothes were in rags; his face was a white, set cast; and when I saw the stare of his eye the shivers trickled down my spine.

I shouted his name, but he never heard. Straight toward me he shuffled, head up, eyes stary, hands hanging in fists at his sides. He walked up to me and right on past without so much as giving me a glance. There was a bump as big as a hen's egg on his left temple. When I saw that, I knew. Tupper marched on, unswerving. Like a somnambulist. As he passed me by I heard him muttering under his breath.

"They were drowned. Noah. The Ark. Gone." A low, shocked whisper.

"He's batty!" I was whispering myself. Whispering and cold. "Crazy. Crazy as a loon!" And finding my legs, I chased that weird figure up the sand. I caught him and held him by the wrist, and he just stood there, staring. He didn't know it when I finally led him along. He opened one fist and stared at the little object in his palm as he walked. The object in his palm, you understand, was a little gold idol!

"**AND THAT,**" said Bradshaw, pausing to empty his hot pipe by tapping it on the ship's rail, "is my story." He tucked the pipe into his pocket, and turned on me with a bemused smile; chuckled.

The young British consular agent at my elbow chuckled, too. After all, it was I who disputed my friend's story. There was Africa—a black shore-line slipping by abeam, and our ship was a reality.

"Some yarn!" I admitted, getting the naturalist by the sleeve. "But, whew! Look here, old man. You don't expect us to believe you actually saw Noah's Ark, to say nothing of the Biblical menagerie and *Noah!* That would be a whopper. Didn't you prepare us for this by quoting that Arab proverb before you started the tale? The proverb about believing only half of what you hear of Africa, and nothing of what you see?"

The naturalist grinned, "Hmmm. Let's suppose a few things. In the first place, there was Camille Caillard, who disappeared in those mountains fifteen years before I got there. A genius. A little cracked on this naturalist game. Suppose he locked himself in those Abyssinian backhills of Gojjam; found that inland lake and settled down for a stay. Good timber in that valley. Say he built himself a floating barn. Say he started stocking it with a collection of specimens. All sorts of specimens in the surrounding forests. Hunter's paradise. What a locale for a naturalist! He stays and stays on. Becomes something of a hermit. Collecting becomes his one passion. Strange mental quirks can come to lonely white men deep in Africa.

"His mob of animals? Listen. The pair of lions were his pets and alive no end. The others? I don't know for sure. They looked live enough in the shadows of that craft's deep hold. But the nyala gazelle that had floated ashore after the storm—I wish I'd examined it more closely. Close scrutiny might have proved it stuffed! Maybe all those other animals were stuffed. Caillard would be a master taxidermist. It's a real art. And he was working at a framework of bones. And there was that deckload of straw.

"But Tupper came along, and I had no chance to examine that nyala. I led Tupper up the beach, and we found our horses where we'd left them. We rode away from that lake. Later we found our guides. Tupper never spoke. All the way out of Abyssinia, out of Africa, back to England he never spoke. The London doctors said he'd get over it. Mental shock to his deep-rooted religion. Aphasia. They told me to keep the gold idol and never let him see it again, and maybe he'd come around. I understand he did, finally. But he didn't recall Abyssinia.

"Getting back to Caillard, remember this. He'd been a goldsmith before he became a collector. That might explain any gold found aboard his 'ark.' Say he carried a few ingots along with him. Something to work on when he had nothing else to do. Maybe, when his mind became deranged by genius or solitude—I'm guessing at it all—he determined to fashion the only specimen he hadn't been able to capture for his collection. I don't know. But it might explain *this*. Look at it."

Bradshaw drew something from his pocket; held it in shut fist. "This sort of brings the story back to the Noah legend again. This makes me wonder if, after all, that really wasn't *the* Ark. Makes me wonder if all of those animals weren't alive. Makes me wonder if that old man wasn't Noah come down through the ages. Noah in person. This makes me wonder. I suppose I'll always wonder. For Abyssinia is Abyssinia, you know. And my Arab proverb doesn't say anything about disbelieving what you can feel! So run your fingers over this. This is the gold idol Tupper was carrying in his fist."

Bradshaw held out his palm. On his palm rested a beautifully carved little idol of solid yellow gold. The idol was carved to represent a dove with its wings poised for flight. A little gold dove, it was. *And in its beak it carried an olive branch!*

# CLAWS

*With smoldering lead and a maudlin song the
Orient trap was baited. And Peter Scarlet—blinded
by heart hunger—swallowed the deadly lure.*

**QUEER BUSINESS WAS** brewing down at Waterfront Willy's Starboard Light Rum Palace, in Penang.

Waterfront Willy, himself, proprietor and maestro behind the bar, wondered what was in the wind. There had been a commotion at the door, a sharp exchange of words. Then a trim little man, boasting an enormous sun helmet and a monumental burst of white whiskers, had strolled into the drinking room, nodded curt greeting, and taken a table in the middle of the floor. Waterfront Willy leaned his pendulous belly against the bar; placidly bent to the shining of a wine glass and the frank study of this newcomer. The dive-keeper's Chinese, Egyptian, Scotch face suddenly beamed a smile of recognition.

"An' it's 'ello to you, Peter Scarlet. What you 'avin' this hevening? You ain't been on this island come long time. Long time since you was 'ere. Down to see some o' th' boys?"

The little American curio-hunter gave a brief nod. "I see you run the same rotten hole you always did, Waterfront. H'm. But the bobbies will get you yet, I reckon. As for me, bring me a bottle of the best wine in the place. Make it good. It's too hot for stiff drinks tonight."

Waterfront Willy moved his spindly legs among kegs and jugs and resurrected a bottle from behind the bar. The dive-keeper was puzzled. He knew this Peter Scarlet. The little American curio-hunter was a recognized figure from Port Said to Karafuto, the Kizil Kum to the Celebes Sea. But he was not a denizen of unsavory dope-halls such as Waterfront Willy knew his Staboard Light Rum Palace to be. The dive-keeper covertly watched his guest, wondering.

The drinking-room was not crowded, for the hour was early. A drunken stoker, with gin and coal-dust in his ears, snored at a corner table. A drunken Tommy spraddled in a chair near the bar, unconscious. They and Waterfront Willy and Peter Scarlet were the only occupants of the low-ceilinged, long room.

Sitting alone in the center of the floor, the little American curio-hunter looked strangely out of place among the speckled tables, the roach-spotted walls, the tawdry tapestries that hung the dancing platform. The dive-owner noted the fact that where Peter Scarlet sat he could watch both the door from the street and the screen-hung inner doors that led to opium dens and gambling corridors. When Waterfront Willy brought the ordered wine the bottle was left untouched.

Behind the bar once more, Waterfront Willy felt he was, himself, under his guest's survey. Shadowed by the broad brim of his sun helmet, Peter Scarlet's cobalt-blue eyes roved the room. Now they studied the brass lamp hanging over his head. Now they watched the door, the man behind the bar, the platform at the room's end. Now they concentrated on the red eye of the black cigar he had jabbed into his teeth. Smoke, purled steadily from the snowy beard, wreathed the peak of the helmet. The strong-fingered brown hands that were noted for the fabulous fortunes they had held and the fabulous speed at drawing certain weapons, tapped calmly on the table-top.

After a long interval, disturbed by the fall of a *chipkilli* from a rafter and the entry and exit of a cat-footed Malay servant, Peter Scarlet looked over to the bar. He pointed a thumb at the screened doors leading to inner rooms.

"Many customers around tonight, Willy?"—tersely.

The Scotch-Chinese-Egyptian made a suave moon of his oily face. "There's a few in, friend. Business *has* been bleedin' slow. I lost me last piano player a while back. But I picked me up a new one off th' beach yesterday. That brings th' gang in. They likes a bit o' music with their glass, yer know. Good bright song an' a weepy one, maybe. This new guy I got can play an' sing fine. You'll see 'em mob in soon as th' music starts. Ones in 'ere now is mostly native. Later comes th' bullies from th' boats. We fills up with a good lively crowd o' buckos about eleven o'clock. You'll see 'em."

Peter Scarlet settled back in his chair, lit another ebony cigar. Evidently he was going to stick around and see them. A little prickle chilled the ruffles at the nape of Waterfront Willy's damp, fat neck as he caught the glint of the curio-hunter's blue eyes. Stony as marble. Flinty. And something informed the dive-keeper that Peter Scarlet was not visiting the Starboard Light Rum Palace on a sight-seeing tour, either. There was a quaint bulge, an obvious protuberance beneath the breast of the little man's trim drill jacket that hinted at the presence of a waiting, ready gun.

**BENDING** his head ever so slightly, the stalwart man peered through a crack in the rattan screen. What he saw brought a smile of satisfaction that tightened his loose-lipped mouth to a sinister carmine line. His winky, porcine eyes—black buttons restive in little cups of blood-sparked hate. The slim smile, as he peered, altered to an ugly leer. His thick, wet, pulpy lower lip drooped to hang open his mouth and reveal a battery of crooked teeth. He moistened his upper lip with a quick tongue, like a boy would lick away a smear of chocolate. He wrinkled his spatulate nose and wrought a scowl on his jutting forehead. Not a pleasant visage with its knife-scar forking across the left cheek, its toss of damp, curly hair, its truculent unkempt chin with the deep black dimple dotting the center. The twisty leer did not enhance its beauty.

"Yah!" whispered the unlovely mouth. "There he be! I knowed as he'd come. There he is. There he sets. I knowed he would. I knowed that letter would fetch 'im; an' he'd stay. He's that kind, th' bleedin', low-life hyena. Looks like he allus did, too. A bleedin' Sandy Claus." The mouth gave vent to a scurrile chuckle. "But it's me who's thinkin' a hour from now he won't be so bleedin' calm an' bleedin' cool. No he won't. Settin' an' waitin', eh? Brave, heh? I reckoned he'd be. Baby! He'll do some smart jumpin' an' hoppin' before this night's gone around!" The mouth panted angrily. "Bloody Judas! After all these years. An' th' time has come at last—"

The man brought his scabrous face away from the screen with a jerk; stood to his full height, lips split in a polluted grin, eyes flickering. Hands in pockets, he teetered back and forth on his heels. His massive shoulders under his ragged cloak shook with silent mirth. His twitching cheeks went the color of new-dug beets. Sweat crawled from the curls straggling down his forehead and rolled slowly down his bulbous nose.

"I got th' bloody little skunk, now," he whispered to himself. "An' baby, how I've got him!" The face mirrored purple hate once more. "Th' bleedin' little truck. Him as done for me a-plenty. Now it's *my* turn. An' ain't I glad I waited. All these years. All these long days an' hours. Me a-humpin' an' crawlin' along. An' now I got me hooks in him at last. I'm thinkin' he ain't never

forgot me, nor he ain't never goin' to, neither. He's gonna remember a lot o' things tonight. *How!*"

Once more the cloaked figure stooped to peek through the
rattan screen; then retreated down the narrow corridor. Like
an evil shade in the dank twilight of the narrow passageway. A
sinister, cloaked shadow that moved with a curious precision—
as if it dragged a dead limb. Silently it moved an inner door
and slid into a feebly lighted room that evidently served as
living quarters.

There was a decrepit iron stove leaning in a corner cluttered
with crockery and fly-hunted scraps of food. Heaps of ragged
garments hung from wall-hooks. A tattered hammock was
slung from corner to corner under the leaky ceiling. On a mat
beneath the hammock crouched what might have been a boy.

A candle sat in a dish full of cigaret stubs at one of the bony
elbows, a red bottle sat at the other. As the cloaked figure
loomed in the doorway, the boy swung the bottle to his lips.
His gaunt throat gurgled. Setting the bottle aside, he wiped a
hand across his dripping lips. The lambent glow of the candle
made his young face into an aged, hollow-eyed mask set atop
a scrawny, unwashed neck. His mouth was old. His flat cheeks
were gray, sunken, smudged with grime. His eyes were sullen
beneath a thatch of curiously colored hair—that rare pink found
in occasional corners of Saxony—that fell across his white
forehead. One would have said he was ill, or addicted to drugs.

The cloaked figure, hands in pockets, stood framed in the
door and grinned. "Yar! At th' wine again, heh? Well, no matter.
Git up off th' mat, Kid. Come along wi' me. I got somethin'
plenty nice to show yer." An elbow under the cloak beckoned.
The black curls nodded. "Somethin' you been wantin' ter see."

**THE BOY** stumbled up from the mat; clapped a frowsy hat
on his head; crept from the room at the man's bidding. The man
quietly led the way down the unlighted corridor; motioned the
boy to the rattan screen. The boy peeked through the crack, his
face twisting.

His companion's crass voice whispered softly in his ear:
"There he be, Kid. Settin' alone right there. There's th' yella
mongoose who put a knife in yer daddy's back an' fired a bullet
into yer sleepin' mother. I told you I'd get him around here fer
you. An' there's yer meat, Kiddo. Him a-sittin' there by hisself.
Middle o' th' room under th' lamp. With th' cheroot in his
bleedin' whiskers. *Him as kilt yer folks.*"

A shudder rustled down the boy's unfed frame. A sudden
fury of blood flushed his face as he withdrew it from the screen.
He glared, panting; made a sudden lunge at his companion;
grabbed at the cloak. "So that's *him*, is it? That's th' guy we been
huntin' fer heh? Th' guy who knifed my dad from behind an'
shot my mother. By Gawd! Gimme th' gun, you. Gimme that
gun! I'll get him right now. I'll shoot off his bloody head fer
him. Where's yer gun—" Tears of rage wiggled down the writhing face. "Gimme that gun, I tell you—"

"Fer th' sake o' Bleedin' Judas!" oathed the man in the cloak,
poking an elbow into the boy's mouth and tramping a heavy
heel across the lad's broken shoe. "Cut th' noise! Wait, you
bloody little fool! Don't mouth it so loud. Not so loud. Wanta
gum everything I been tryin' so long to fix fer yuh? Wanta spoil
yer chance? Hush quiet, an' do as I tells. Do as we been plannin'.
Now do as I says. Rummage in me left pocket an' git out me
automatic. Left hand pocket, see? Got it? Good. Now ram it
inta yer pants, an' keep it there as I says. Now lissen, you. When
you shoots this ole buzzard you gotta do it quick an' neat an'
plenty, see? I got th' gat all loaded fer yuh. Th' ole skunk won't
be armed, but yuh gotta catch him quick, see? First three shots.
You gettin' me? Now yer gonna do it as I says, ain't you? Like
we planned?"

"I'd like to pop him now," the boy snarled thickly, juggling
the automatic he had dug from his companion's cloak. "I'd like
to shoot his blood-slopped mug off him right where he sets!
Th' lousy hound! Murdered my folks, did he? I'd like to walk
right out there an' blow away his eyes! I—"

"Can it!" snapped the other. "Don't be a bloody jackass. We

been waitin' too long fer this chance t' have it spoilt by no fool moves. I'd shoot him from behind this screen, myself, only you knows I can't noways handle a small gun. I'd git him with me shotgun, only you wants him fer yerself, don't yuh? Yar! Then do as I says. What yuh think I got ya this job an' all fer? What yuh think I cooked up this plant fer? So's yuh could git th' hound an' git him right. An' not have th' police stringin' yuh up by yer throat. Now you listen to me!"

**HE PUT** his pulpy lips close to the boy's ear. "When Waterfront Willy comes t' yer room an' asks yuh to come out an' do yer piano playin', you walks out to that stage an' goes to th' piano, see? Like yuh usually does. Play as allus. A bleedin' tune er two. While y're up there git that guy located in your mind, see? Have your gun hand ready t' dive, an' spot him where he's settin'. You know right where he sets from where you set, so's yuh can swing on yer stool an' plant lead in his guts an' head. He ain't far from yuh, an' with my automatic yuh can't never miss, see? Now y're playin' yer piana an' singin'. Have th' top o' th' piana lifted. *I'm* hidin' back here with me shotgun.

"You plays a bit, then wallers inta yer sad-eyed song like Waterfront Willy asks fer this aft. Sing th' piece yuh was doin' up in Jonsey's place in Algiers. Sing that there *Jest a Song At Twilight*. That has the bloody customers weepin', see? That's my signal, see? Th' last note o' that song. When y're on th' last note, I lets fly an' pops out th' lamp. Second my gun whams, you whips around, fires fast an' empties yer gat inta this whitewhiskered bloke who's done yuh dirt. Then, quicker'n wink, yuh drops yer cannon inta th' piana, see? Room's dark an' everybody's hollerin' an' flounderin'. Time they get a light on, you're outa there. Nobody guesses nor sees it was you. You ain't got no gun. You beats it outa there in a jiffy, an' they ain't a thing against yuh. It goes off slick as soap." The man grinned wryly. "O' course *I* could git him. I could pop off his nut, myself, easy as pie. But I reckoned *you'd* want t' do it yerself—"

"He's *mine!*" the boy raged out through clenched teeth. *"I'm* gonna kill him. This yella skunk is fer me, see? It was my folks he done in, an' I'm gonna do him. I'll work it like you planned. Maybe yer idea is best. But let me put th' bullets inta him. Don't you dare go an' plug him! I wanna croak him, myself. Shoot out th' light fer me, but if—"

"All right. All right," the man soothed through his leer. "He's yours to croak. He ain't nothing to me. All I been doin' is just helpin' you locate him an' get him planted, tha's all. I knowed yer folks, an' yer ma was a friend o' mine. I knowed 'em well, yer ma an' yer dad." He smiled thinly. "Like I been tellin' you, right along. Now it's up to you."

Again the boy bent to peer through the rattan screen. "He's still settin' there, th' little rat. I'll croak him, all right. Don't worry none about me missin'. I'll plug his eyes—"

"Sure you will," snarled the man. "Cos he done in yer folks. Now beat it! An' don't forget! Sing five or six songs. Then yer weepy number, see? Then as you ends it I smashes th' light. Then quick as scat you turns an' shoots. Drop yer gun in th' piana—scoot. Got me? Now git outa here an' wait!"

Muttering oaths, the boy scurried up the corridor. The cloaked man watched him go; wet his lips with his tongue; grinned like a skull. Then he pushed his face against the screen, beady eyes to the crack, and whispered to himself: "So it's comin' to yer at last, me fine bully. Few minutes, now. An' then ain't you gonna suffer? *How!* How y're gonna suffer! Baby! Guess I didn't crack th' ole nozzle figgerin' all these years fer nothin'. You done me plenty, little skunk, an' now it's comin' back to yuh. All I hafta do is pop that lantern, an' git it in th' right spot. An' th' last note is what does it. That's what does fer *you!* I goes now an' gits me shotgun. An' th' *last note* is what fixes you!"

He glared through the rattan screen.

**THE HINDU** chattered, and Wilhelm Schneider, the beery Dutch artist from Islamahad chattered. The Hindu waved his skinny hands like crazy little bats under the expatriate Dutchman's numerous chins. Wilhelm Schneider brought a score of goodly Rhineland oaths up from his several stomachs, trapped the Hindu's skinny wrists, and panted into the spouting native face. Finally the overwrought gentleman from India ended his wild speech, and the fat artist from Islamahad began to run.

Wilhelm Schneider ran; which was unusual for one so fat. His heels pounded the dust to smoke. Sweat poured in rivulets from the band of his sun-helmet. His linen suiting flapped like a distress signal on his corpulent frame as he panted down the palm-bordered lane, up the broad avenue where rickshaws and motors flickered through the warm night. Across a square and up a street and across a lawn to a hotel veranda. Like an elephant stampeding from a legion of mice. The Malay gardener watched the fat figure race by, and wondered. The artist *tuan* and his friend of the great white beard and his friend of the long shanks stayed often at the hotel; but never had the gardener seen the fat one run so. Evil spirits must be afoot!

Holmes Bradshaw, the gaunt Kelantan naturalist, had much the same idea as he saw his fat friend charging up the veranda steps. He swung out of his chair, and rapped the ashes from his pipe as the Dutchman loomed, gasping, across the porch.

"What ho, old top?" the naturalist greeted. "I say, why the race, and from whom? You look as if you'd been trying out for the Olympic Ga—"

"*Gott im Himmel!*" panted the artist, mopping water from his three chins. "This iss no time for the jest, Bradshaw! *Nein!* What do you t'ink! *Ja!* Trouble? I am one monkey if there iss not trouble for us tonight. So! Listen! Just now by our club I meet Peter Scarlet's boy, Kundoo. He is upset! That Hindu is one excited boy. He is so! And with a good reason! Do you guess what he told me? He runs up to me squeaking like mice. He tells me there is something in the air wrong with Peter. His gods and his eyes tell him it. He said he had met Peter Scarlet two hours before going into this Waterfront Willy's place. You know Waterfront Willy's place? That dive by the wharfs! *Ja!* That hole that would turn your soul into Swiss cheese. That is the place.

"And Kundoo saw Peter go in there. Kundoo wass coming out. He tries to argue with Peter about going in, but the curio-hunter does not listen. Kundoo says Peter looks very excited. Peter will not listen, and he gets mad and cuffs the Hindu and tells him to clear away! Perhaps, thinks Kundoo, Peter Scarlet only goes in for a drink. The Hindu waits by the door. He iss a good boy, that Hindu. He waits one hour. He waits two. Our friend does not come out. Then Kundoo iss scared. He runs over to the club to tell somebody. He finds me and I run back here to the hotel to get my gun and find you. *Ja!* Shades of Friedrich Wilhelm! I believe there iss something wrong with Peter Scarlet. I am going to this Starboard Light of a Rum Palace. We cannot—"

"You bet we can't!" snapped the naturalist "Wonder what old Peter is doing in a cut-throat joint like that?" He fingered his long chin reflectively. "Come to think of it, I saw the old boy as he was leaving the hotel. He seemed a bit bothered and in a hurry. Queer. We can't let him hang around a dump like that alone. That Waterfront Willy's is the lousiest dive on th' China Coast or anywhere. I'll just grab my gat and mosey down there with you. If there's anything happened to Peter we'll shoot the place full of holes an' tell the police afterwards. But I don't think we need worry much," he amended. "The curio-hunter is a master hand at taking care of himself. And you know what he is with a gat—"

**BUT THE** gaunt Kelantan naturalist was worried. So was Wilhelm Schneider. Why was the curio-hunter spending an evening in an unsavory dope den like the Starboard Light Rum Palace? They knew—though Peter Scarlet was ever reticent about such matters—that the little curio-hunter owned several enemies who would have been only too glad to drive knives into his spine. Bradshaw mentioned this as he hustled to his room. The Dutchman cursed and mopped his face, bustling off to get an automatic.

With guns in snug holsters under their jackets, the two then hailed a rickshaw and rolled speedily down to the native quarter. On foot they hurried down the square bordered by the little houses where the lights were dim, down through the shadowy Chinese Quarter alive with flickery lamps and the nauseous squealing of pigs in the slaughter pens, to the waterfront. Here they wove way down long wharfs where fences of masts and foreign funnels spiked against a tropic sky flashing with low, hot stars.

From the distance they could see the pernicious green glow of the ship's lantern marking the entry of the Starboard Light Rum Palace. The one-story ramshackle edifice rambled along the edge of a rotting wharf. The slop of green water seeped up through the decaying planks under foot. Schneider and Bradshaw picked way over coiled hawsers and shore-lines, cursing. As they neared the glow of the green ship's lantern that so aptly reflected the poisonous locale, they were treated to a burst of noise. A roaring, drunken chant of the sea.

The rusty, tin-walled warehouses crouching on either side of Waterfront Willy's echoed to the clash of the ribald music drifting through the green-hazed door. Hands were hammering a tinny, outcast piano. Thick red throats were bellowing the words of the ditty. Heavy boots tramped; mugs thumped to beat cadent time.

> While I'm floatin' down Soul' Street one day I did spy—
> A sweet littul ladeee as to-ook my eye—

*"Ach, der lieber Gott!"* snorted Wilhelm Schneider, his face a red moon peering over the raucous threshold into the smoke-fogged, roaring chamber within. "Here iss one *verdammt* scorpion's nest or I am a Spaniard. To go in here—it is, Bradshaw, like strolling into hell, eh?" Then his pudgy fingers caught the naturalist's sleeve. *"Himmel! Look!* There iss Peter! In the very center of the room. He iss alone at a table. For why? Look at him! Come—we go and sit with him!"

"Good Lord!" exclaimed Bradshaw, staring. "What the devil is he doing here, anyhow? Look at the gang of cut-throats packing this hole. That rotten bunch of Greek sailors over there. That mob of stewed Limy stokers. Half-breeds. Dope hounds. Never saw a worse crew in my life. I'm after you, Schneider. We can't let Peter fool around alone in a sink like this. Lead away to his table. I'm with you."

**PANTING,** elbowing officiously, the beery Dutchman shoved through the crowd blocked about the bar. Whisky-reddened eyes leered. Bearded mouths spat insults. But the Dutchman shoved away, pushed a path through the clutter of chairs and tables, stepped over spraddling legs, kicked a Malay waiter to one side, tramped on a lady's boot, and brought up at Peter Scarlet's chair. The little American curio-hunter looked up with an oath of surprise; half rose from his seat.

"I say! It's Schneider and Bradshaw. Now what the devil!" His blue eyes frowned. "You two! Who—So that rascally boy of mine told you I was down here, didn't he? Told on me, eh? I'll give it to Kundoo for this! I didn't want anybody around. You—I can't have you here, old chaps. You birds will have to clear out. I want to be alone, and—"

Nodding, Holmes Bradshaw slipped into a chair, calmly crossed his knees. The Dutchman from the Islamahad dropped into the remaining chair, leaned elbows on the table, shook his head. "You see, we don't stir," chuckled the naturalist. "We don't move, old top."

"We don't move an inch!" agreed the Dutchman stubbornly. "No sir. We ain't going to leave our friend sitting in this dope hell by himself alone. What are you doing, Peter? Why iss this? There iss some bad trouble, I think."

Schneider wrinkled his forehead with a frown, lowered his voice and nudged the curio-hunter's arm. "You are carrying your gun, too," he accused; with no danger of being overheard, for the room was still squalling out the dubious virtues of Miss O'Pimple. "You carry your automatic. For what, Peter? *Gott!* You can't stay in this place by yourself. We cannot let you. Tell us about it. Your two best friends. We will not go away. *Nein!* Not until we learn why you are here."

The little curio-hunter glared at the men across the table from him, then a smile brightened his blue eyes and brought crimson patches to his cheeks. Darting a piercing glance around the room, another at his wrist-dial, he leaned across the table.

"All right," he said quietly. "It was white of you to come down. I might tell you that if you stay there may be grave danger for both of you. You'll stay, will you? Then," he said abruptly, "I'll tell you what's up. As much as I can anyway—" He glanced quickly about him again. The room was turbid with blue smoke; vibrating with noise. "Rotten racket, eh? Rotten place for a *rendezvous?*"

Bradshaw cursed saliently. "Rendezvous! With who? Peter, what's up? You *are* packing your gun. I can see it plain as anything—"

The curio-hunter smiled sternly, stabbed his whiskers with a fresh cigar. "You chaps have known me for years. Yet, you haven't. I reckon you been wondering why I've been traipsing over the Orient. Always on the go. I never told you, but I guess you've known I wasn't really hunting trinkets. Now I'll tell you a story. I'll make it short because it's mighty ugly. But I think you lads might as well know it, after all."

Naturalist and Dutch artist sat up; looked at one another. Their friend's voice had come like a knife-blade. They had never heard him talk like that before. They leaned forward. Ropes of smoke reeled about Scarlet's head. His eyes had become icy blue china. His voice cut just loud enough for them to hear above the song roared out by the room.

> "Oh, I sailed th' seas fer thirty years,
>     Fer thirty years or more!
> But I never seen a cabbage head
>     With ears on it before!"

The room was bellowing. The boy at the derelict piano—a derelict himself—was pounding furiously, shoulders hunched, fingers beating venomously on the keys, feet jamming the pedals, hat rammed over his ears. The room shook with sound. But Holmes Bradshaw and Wilhelm Schneider could only hear Peter Scarlet's steel voice.

"**I CAME** East when I was twenty. Went home at forty and married and brought my wife back to Hongkong with me. Shipping business, in those days. Export." A short sigh blew smoke from his white beard. "I'll cut it short, it's so rotten. I can see you're going to tell me I needn't tell it if it's painful. It is. But I want you to know. I've got a queer hunch that maybe tonight—

"Any way, my wife's son was born the day we got to Hong-kong. A year later my wife and the baby were kidnaped. Stolen by a renegade. A half-Spanish, half-English adventurer. Castor was his name. An utter buzzard. Police called him Claws Castor. You see, he—he didn't have any hands. Just a steel hook for each hand."

Peter Scarlet's voice shook. He brushed mist from his forehead. "This monster asked forty thousand pounds for the return of the wife and baby. Said he'd shoot 'em both and send 'em back to me in a week if I didn't send the money he demanded. I hadn't an available penny. I didn't put it past him killing the girl and the baby, and I tried like hell to raise it. Couldn't get it." Scarlet coughed. "My wife and baby were shot. He sent them to me by a rickshaw man who thought they were bundles of laundry—"

"*Got im himmel!*" sobbed the Dutchman. Bradshaw's angular face was of chalk.

The curio-hunter went on: "I got up a gang. I hounded that devil. Hounded him! And I trailed and caught him way up on the Lena River after a terrible, terrible chase. I was frenzied; almost mad. We trapped him alone in a deserted hut, abandoned by his gang. Left to starve and freeze. But he wasn't by any means dead, the rotten murderer. He put up a stiff fight. Good with a shotgun. I ordered my men back, and I went into that hut after him with a revolver in one hand and an axe in the other. Heaven couldn't have stopped me. I was insane. You see, he'd been so cold-blooded about my wife and—"

"*Lieber Gott!*" Schneider, the beery artist mopped his chins desperately. "This iss one *verdammt* awful story, Peter. I hope you fixed that *hund!*"

"I chopped off his right leg," growled the curio-hunter. "And let him alone to die. It seems he didn't. Three years later I got a letter signed Claws—typed. It said, 'I am still alive. So is your kid. Keep an eye out for us. Claws.' He had, by his claim, sent me someone else's baby. My boy lived. I hunted. I've been hunting. Five years later came the same note, again. On Christmas day. Another six years ago. They may have been fakes. About my boy, anyway. God, how I've hoped they were. But I went on searching. No trace."

Now Peter Scarlet's voice was granite and edged with steel that carved through the uproar. "But this afternoon came a note. It said: 'Be in Waterfront Willy's tonight from eight until one o'clock. Sit in the middle of the room. You will see something that is very, very sure to interest you.' That was all. No signature." Peter Scarlet's eyes narrowed. "But it was typed." A mirthless chuckle escaped his beard. His fingers inched over the bulge on his breast. "I'm here. It's half past eleven."

Wilhelm Schneider gulped. Bradshaw said nothing. The naturalist was pale, and warm sweat glistened on his cheeks. Peter Scarlet leaned back in his chair, studying the eye of his cigar. The room had quieted. Hoarse voices had choked out, and the trio at the center table became aware that the creature at the piano on the stage—a wretched beach boy from all appearances—was playing and singing a solo.

He sang with his eyes shifting at the crowd, his raw voice sawing out the melody. Waterfront Willy's Starboard Light Rum Palace had hedged into a maudlin mood, green as the lamp over its entry. A woman at a corner table with a floppy hat wearing a peacock had a lace kerchief to her jaded nose. A bull-necked Irishman at the bar sniffed audibly. The scrawny youth at the piano sang huskily.

*"Jest a song at Tuh-wi-light—"*

**HE CAUGHT** off his hat with a theatric gesture as he lingered on the note. The towsled sheaf of pink hair fell across his forehead, and his face was wet.

*"Still to us at tuh-wi-light—"* (And now Peter Scarlet, the little American curio-hunter, was half out of his chair; fingers gripping the rim of the table.) *"Comes love's ole songgg—"* sang the wretched pianist. (And Peter Scarlet was on his feet, glaring, face the color of snow.) The soloist finished his number slowly: *"Comes—luhuv's—suhweet sawng—"*

*Wham!* A fierce, blatant gunshot that seemed to come from one of the screened doors leading to an inner room. The drinking den clattered with crashing echo. The lamp hanging from the center of the ceiling rocked to and fro, flickered, dimmed. But it *did not go out.*

At the instant of the shot, the boy at the piano had whirled on his stool, opened fire with an automatic in his fist.

*Wham! Wham!*

Jets of vermilion flame streaked from the muzzle of his gun. Straight at the face of Peter Scarlet who stood in the center of the floor. The room shrieked, tables went over, heads ducked. Bradshaw bounced to his feet, automatic in fist. Wilhelm Schneider bobbed up with a furious oath.

The naturalist's gun exploded. But the bullet did not speed at the boy. With a sudden punch, Peter Scarlet had turned Bradshaw's gun aside, and the bullet streaked into the ceiling. The Dutchman's weapon bellowed. But Peter Scarlet's had fired at the same instant. The little curio-hunter's bullet struck Schneider's gun. The Dutchman's automatic sailed from his hand, its bullet whizzing across the room and plucking feathers from the peacock in the woman's hat.

The boy on the stage was cursing wildly, shooting with loud cries. He sped his fourth shot straight at the curio-hunter. His fifth shot. Peter Scarlet was pouncing at him. His sixth shot, almost into the curio-hunter's beard. Peter Scarlet did not fall. Bounding to the platform, the curio-hunter brought his gun-butt down with a furious tap across the boy's jaw. The boy fell across his stool like a sack of wet grain. Peter Scarlet stumbled to his knees.

Waterfront Willy was screaming. The lamp had flared up once more, found the low-ceiled room filled with yells, shouts, white faces, wreathing wisps of pungent powder smoke. Heads came out from under tables, from behind the bar, from behind door screens. Waterfront Willy was howling in Chinese, Egyptian and Scotch. Holmes Bradshaw, the gaunt Kelantan naturalist, charged forward cursing grandly. Snorting stiff oaths and waving a numb fist, the Dutchman stumbled at Bradshaw's heels. On the platform they found Peter Scarlet on his knees, peering into the face of the unconscious boy limp in his arms. The Dutchman and the naturalist stared wide-eyed.

"Kid!" Peter Scarlet was saying softly. "Kid. Kid—"

**"HERR GOTT!"** exploded Schneider. "It iss, Peter, one miracle you are alive. He fired right into your face. My! how did he miss? And why did you shoot the gun from my fingers so? Shades of Von Bismarck!"

"I had him dropped!" echoed Bradshaw. "You flung me off my aim. I say, Peter—why—he— How'd he ever miss you, and—"

The curio-hunter laid down his limp burden, picked up the boy's automatic and ejected a shell. "He didn't miss," said Scarlet in a low tone. "His gun was loaded with blanks. See? And—and I didn't want to shoot him. I—I recognized him when he took his hat off. It's *him*. I—he's got *her* hair! Just like hers, and I knew it when—"

A commotion at the door under the green light. Malay boy bustling forward with a message for a Peter Scarlet. Waterfront Willy pushing through the seething crowd with a white slip in his hand, voice spouting oaths.

"Peter Scarlet! A note fer yuh! Someone outside give it to th' Malay, couple minutes ago. Told him t' bring it to yuh here. An' lemme git my hands on that lousy, bleedin' piana player, an' I'll—"

"Wait. Keep this mob back!" The curio-hunter took the neatly folded note. It was carefully typed, and read:

DEAR PETER SCARLET:

The dopy brat you have just shot to death is your own son. I framed him with blanks in his gun, framed him about the light, so's he'd turn and pot at you. And, of course, you being such a lightning shot and all, yes? But he is your own brat, and you killed him. He's got a birthmark under his arm that proves it; the other baby was faked. Too bad to kill your own boy. Sorry. Of course, I loved the brat. As for you, I love you, too. I could have dropped you tonight, myself, but I'm saving you for something better than an easy bullet. Hope you enjoy the funeral, Mister Fast Shot. Planning to see you soon. Have a good funeral for your boy.

Yours affectionately,
CLAWS CASTOR.

Clutching the unconscious wasted frame of the boy in his arms, Peter Scarlet let a savage laugh burst from his heard. "Framed us, eh? Thought I'd shoot my own son. But I recognized him too soon. He didn't remember the boy's hair was like his mother's. Funeral, eh? Funeral! The only funeral I'll be seeing soon is one for Claws Castor."

He gazed warmly down on the bloodless, thin face framed by the swollen jaw and the toss of pink hair.

"My son and I will attend it together!"

### The Story Behind "Claws"

We were talking to Theodore Roscoe, the author of "Claws," the other day and he began yarning about a few of the picturesque hombres he'd run across in the far places. Incidentally, he remarked that he gets a real kick out of using them in his stories. Some of them like it; others are probably gunning for him.

It sounded like good stuff to us. So we asked him to give us the low-down on the cast of "Claws." Here's what he wrote:

The man, Claws, of the prong hands, wooden leg and black cloak is a purely fictitious character, but the story of Peter Scarlet's search for his abducted son is founded on fact.

When my father was roaming down Singapore way, he made the acquaintance of a collector much on the order of Peter Scarlet, the little American curio-hunter. This collector (name withheld because he may still exist) had beaten a path down the China Coast, over Malaya, half across India and back in the hopes of locating a son kidnapped in Shanghai.

Supposedly, the boy was taken as revenge on the father, as the father continued to receive anonymous letters concerning the lad's whereabouts and welfare. He received three or four of them, I believe, in as many years. They may have been penned by the hoodlums and freaks who usually follow up such a notorious affair; or they may have been the work of a fiend.

At any rate, they set the little man off on frantic wild-goose chases, though many of his friends did not know the story and thought him a little daft. Unhappily, when my father knew him he had not as yet located the boy, who must have grown to young manhood by that time.

As for Waterfront Willy's Starboard Light Rum Palace, I have been in the place. It was, however, on the North African coast, and only needed a little transplanting to Penang. The fat Dutch artist of the yarn is a character taken from life. He is no longer Out East, but spends his time between Paris and New York painting magazine covers of Oriental dancing girls and whatnot. The Bradshaw of the story has just left my home town to take up a post in Rio Janeiro. His name is Bradshaw, too, and he likes to read about himself in *Action Stories.*

So most of the characters in the Scarlet series have been yanked from life. All save Claws, himself. And we expect to run into *him* some day.

THEODORE ROSCOE.

# THE RUBY OF SURATAN SINGH

*All the East knew the legend of that
fugitive Indian prince and his treasure; but
Bradshaw, the naturalist, found the legend
come alive before his popping eyes*

**"RIOTING IN CALCUTTA!** Mob Storms Bazaar! Natives Stone Fire and Police Brigades! Many Injured!"

Bradshaw let the *Daily Mail* slip from his fingers; and the headlines yelled up at me from the floor. The naturalist shook his head.

"Poor old India," he said, staring off across the Malacca Strait toward that horizon beyond which she lay. A westering sun was nesting there, gilding the tousled cloud-tips with a light that enameled red the water of our bay. The half-glow found a frown on Bradshaw's face. He sighed.

"Poor old India. She can't seem to understand. She can't seem to be understood. So she's rioting again."

"Trouble," I worried, "for Britain."

He agreed. "India's restless. Britain has done wonders for her. Educated, doctored, fostered, renovated her. But Britain rules her. The father does everything for the kid; but what kid doesn't yearn for the day when he can paddle his own canoe? India's a nervous, hysterical, overgrown child, with all the fever of any other child born in tropic sunshine and malaria. Needs a ruling hand to raise her properly, but is too proud to think so. Poor kid."

"Is that what lies behind this?" I queried, pointing at the newspaper bearing its message of disturbance and alarm.

"I'll tell you what's behind it!" The naturalist's lean hands went seeking into his jacket, and extracted a much-weathered

*"I will show you
the lost trail,"
muttered the hag.*

Kalabash. "I'll tell you," he repeated, when his teeth were leaking pipe-smoke. "And I may get across my idea. But the idea's incidental. The story's the thing. I might say, you're the first chap I ever told it to; and I wouldn't tell it now if we weren't alone on this veranda, if you hadn't seen North India for yourself, and if it didn't seem to fit in. And you'll have to believe it, old man, because it actually happened to *me*. You won't want to believe it, though, because it's the story of the ruby of Suratan Singh!"

"The ruby of Suratan Singh!" I gasped. "Good Lord, you aren't going to tell me you know anything about *that* thing!"

"I know *all* about it," he nodded.

And this is the story he told me:

**QUEER** how legends get under way, how far they travel, how fat they grow. Take this story of Suratan's vast treasure. First time I heard about it was in the opera house in Warren, Ohio. The speaker had sideburns and stereopticon slides and a lecture on India; and when he orated about Suratan making his getaway after leaving that astonishing message to his satrap brother, every kid in Warren, Ohio, was ready to run away and find the Himalaya Mountains.

Few years later I was steaming out of New York Harbor, listening to an old missionary enchant the smoke-room with the same yarn. Between Marseilles and Aden I heard the tale thirteen times, each time getting better and more authentic. After some years out here, I got so used to the story that I told it a couple of times myself, planned thirty times to cash in on it, and finally forgot it. Every adventurer who'd cut his sign on the East-smitten trail between Hadramaut and the Kurils had taken a shot at locating that ruby.

According to legend, though, that ruby should have been easy to find as the rising sun. The boys between Aden and China claimed the stone was as big as a fist. This was substantiated by the assertion that no Hindu would have risked his life to carry off a smaller and less precious piece of treasure. China Coast logic. Certainly the terrified Suratan had made a gargantuan effort to save himself and his fortune.

It must have taken some mighty unusual driving-force to get that fellow through the British line in those gory days. You remember the story. The Sepoy Rebellion had burst like a bomb. The native troops had mutinied from one end of the land to the other, and in that particular July of 1857 the country was knee-deep in blood of massacred whites.

Nana Sahib, the red rajah, had just pulled off his horrible Cawnpore slaughter and was making his escape into the hills. The British under Havelock were after him, hot-foot, wild with sorrow and rage. It would go damned hard with the rebel who was caught by those infuriated British soldiers.

It looked as if one Suratan Singh, prince of Rohilkhand, was going to be one such. He was a Hindu Brahmin of reputed wealth and the usual bad habits. He ruled an unruly corner of India, and he'd loaned some of his household troops to the ineffable Nana Sahib, which chalked him up in red ink for the British. The raging British soldiers pushed fast up into Suratan

Singh's province, and it wasn't long before a detachment of 78th Highlanders had surrounded a little mud house in which the luckless Hindu was known to be hiding.

You can fancy things looked black for that nabob. The Scotchmen closing in on him had seen the bodies of mutilated white women, and they weren't going to coddle a man who'd loaned his troops to Nana Sahib. They were out for the head of Suratan Singh and meant to get it.

They didn't get it. Night came on just as they closed in on the little mud house, and they got there in time to find the bird had flown. Heaven only knows how that Hindu got himself through the ring of fierce Highlanders. But the only thing they found in the little mud room was a note scratched on a piece of leather. Suratan had written and signed the message in Hindee characters. It was addressed to his brother, a satrap in the adjacent province.

The message said Suratan was commending his soul to the Vedic gods and was going to attempt a get-away into the hills. It also mentioned the fact that he was taking with him the one thing he valued most:

"I carry with me my most precious treasure—my most precious ruby." His very words. Signed: Suratan Singh.

**THE CHEATED** Highlanders started after that slippery Hindu like tigers after a pig. They found his footprints when the moon came up, and they followed fast. But the Hindu was going like a wind. Through forty miles of *terai* jungle his tracks led those Highlanders.

Forty terrible miles through slough and upland swamp, bracken and brier-brush, up, down, back, around the Hindu's trail dragged; and that squad of Highlanders chased him. Night and day, for hours on end, they dogged his track, expecting every next step to bring them on the exhausted fugitive. Suratan held the lead. Then his trail thinned out in a tangle of Himalayan cañons. The exhausted Highlanders lost the track. They left three of their number to find it. The three were never seen or heard of again. Neither was Suratan Singh.

There you have the story of the disappearance of Suratan Singh and his precious ruby. The Highlanders who chased him and left three to go to certain death in the wilds had wanted him for his head. But after the Indian Mutiny blew over, the chase after Suratan Singh started again, and those who pursued his trail wanted something else. They wanted that gem. The story spread like contagion. Its truth was established by the message Suratan had scratched to his brother on that chunk of leather. Doomed men don't lie.

Stories started to float. The fugitive nabob had owned an enormous fortune before the Rebellion. His jewels had been famous from Nepal to Baluchistan. This ruby he had picked out of the lot and carried with him on his flight must have been priceless, beyond value. Every man and boy in the hills started to hunt Suratan's trail. Beach combers and pedants, scientists and sailors from the seven seas hit for that patch of Himalaya jungle where Suratan had vanished with his gem.

Though it clipped off some of the details, time hasn't dulled the legend; to-day it's bright as ship's brass. That's why my heart gave a jump, skip and hop when, at the end of my first five years in South India, I got a letter from the Museum of Natural History in New York dispatching me to North India after specimens.

The letter ordered me to the border of Nepal, where I was to bag a pair of armored rhinoceroses. On the way, I knew I'd pass right through the village where, some forty years before, Suratan Singh with his treasure had started his dash for the hills.

I never got them their rhinos.

**I WAS** traveling along the road into Lukunpore when I heard the sound that stood the hair straight up on my head. Did you ever hear the dream-call of a person suffering a nightmare? It's a sound that tickles your spine. Well, that's what I heard—a weird sort of whoo-hoo-hooing, baying up from a ravine below me. The sun had started to drop behind the hills and an amber twilight lay among the mangroves patrolling the trail. That ghostly ululation wasn't nice to hear in an Asian dusk.

"What's that?" I barked at my native boys. My guide, a big fellow wearing nothing but a breech-clout and a magenta blossom behind his left ear, poked a finger at the yawning ravine. At first I was too startled to see anything. Then my eyes worked through the purple shadows and I saw something. A rag, a bone and a hank of hair were knotted together in a ragged thorn-bush halfway down the ravine.

The rag, bone and hair-hank wriggled in the thorns and voiced that weird dream-wail, and at first I thought it was live bait set out to decoy leopards. It was live leopard-bait, all right, but not the kind a hunter would use. I began to see it was an old woman.

She'd fallen off the trail and tumbled into the ravine and caught herself helpless in that clump of thorn. So I started down after her, good Samaritan fashion. The steep gully was nasty with brier, and it was a job getting down to her in that thick darkness.

I didn't get there any too soon. Just as I reached her thorn-trap a shadow slithered along the bottom of the ravine and I caught a glimpse of baleful yellow eyes. No wonder that old woman had hooted like a banshee.

Getting her out of that thorn and up that ravine-wall was a task for Hercules, but I did it. When I got her in my arms I had the creeps. The creature was a living mummy. She was lighter than paper, or I'd never have hoisted her up to the trail. A moon was wheeling in the sky when I finally deposited my burden in the dust of the path, and she lay there gasping like a fish.

My hill-boys spat in disgust. The white *sahib* had wasted his time. This old woman was a *mihtrani*. Sweeper-caste. Lowest of the low. Better to have left her to the leopards.

After I took a good look at the lady I concluded it would have taken a mighty hungry leopard to eat her. There was nothing much to eat. She was nothing but strips of leather hung together by bone, rail-thin, old and sin-ugly. Her hair was a wisp and her teeth only a memory in a caved-in mouth. But the eyes in her withered skull were like fanned embers and she found a voice in her corded neck to tell me her right arm was broken. Marveling that the old brown creature hadn't been broken in half by her fall, I pulled the thorns from my own person and got to work.

A naturalist has to be everything under the sun, including a taxidermist and a doctor. I always carried a medical kit with me; and I managed to set her snapped arm with a splint. My boys looked on in high disdain, spitting copious quids at the path. But the old woman never uttered a groan as I tinkered with her arm, and she got to her feet by herself.

Good Lord! Standing there in the moonlight she was older than ever. Shriveled and skinny, with legs like pipestems and a head like a dried mango, she was nothing but a shadow from the past. Surely the next puff of wind would dust her away.

But the wind came along and she was still there; moreover she spoke, again, to prove reality. She spoke words of difficult hill-dialect, croaking them out through her gums, but I caught them all right, and they gave me a start. For: "Tell me what you want," she said, "and I'll give it to you."

You can imagine I hadn't expected to hear anything like that. If I'd expected anything at all it was a dour word of thanks and to see her pad off down the trail, cursing. "What do you mean?" I asked.

She pointed a crooked finger. "You were going to Lukunpore and thence to find the lost trail," she cawed. "All the white *sahibs* who travel this path look for the lost trail of Suratan Singh. I do not know why, but it is so."

I fumbled with her speech, and then remembered. Of course. Lukunpore was the town where Suratan Singh had started his fadeaway to the mountains. No doubt this old *mihtrani* woman thought I was one of the treasure-hunters seeking the fabulous ruby. I laughed and shook my head, but she gave me a stare from those ember eyes of hers and said something that slapped the wind right out of me.

"If you want the way of the trail," she said, "I will give it to you."

"You mean," I blurted, "you can show me where Suratan took his treasure? You mean—"

"You have been kind to me," the ancient said, and her voice was an echo from a yesterday. "I know where Suratan went because I followed him like the soldiers. I can show you where Suratan lies!"

"Is his treasure still there?" I gasped; and she nodded:

"Do you want to see it?"

**WELL,** you could have knocked me flat with a pinfeather! Here was this crone, this incredible old witch whom chance had let me save from ruining a leopard's digestion, asking me if I wanted to see the spot where Suratan's treasure lay. As if she could show me the pot of gold at rainbow's end if I'd like her to pull it out of a plug hat. Sort of nonchalant.

I thought of the thousand and one lusty devils who'd fought and scraped and trailed all over hell and died trying to find Suratan Singh's track. Then I let out a hyena's laugh. My hill-boys thought that ancient crone had put a curse on me, and they backed away uneasily.

I guess they were right. I continued laughing, but I laughed a little too long.

That old *mihtrani* witch got a claw on my arm. "The white *sahib* thinks I speak untruth!" she snarled. "Then listen!"

I found myself listening. I couldn't do anything else. I sat on a bowlder at the edge of the path and the old woman squatted in front of me, telling a story. Her story was hampered because she only had one hand she could gesture with, but she did mighty well, just the same. The moonlight made her a genie;

and little, jungle-perfumed winds came whispering out of the sky to tell me she was telling me the truth.

She spoke in a guttural dialect mixed up with a lot of Pushtu and Oriental epigram, some of which I couldn't unravel, but I got the main points of the story, don't forget it.

She told me the story of Suratan's fadeaway with the treasure—the story I'd heard a thousand times before. But my ears stuck out stiff as tin. She had the edge on this legend, all right. She'd been *in* it.

To start with, she told me she was two hundred years old; so I knocked off a hundred years for the sake of accuracy, and then saw she could have been a girl back in 1857 when Suratan hid in that mud house, waiting for the Scotties to finish him.

What do you think? She, herself, had been hiding behind a *peepul* tree, watching the whole affair. She knew Suratan was in the mud house, and she saw the tall Highlanders manufacture their ring of bayonets and start to close in.

That old *mihtrani* woman made me see the thing as she saw it, then. I could see the glint of the bayonets, the set faces of the angry Scots under their high shakoes, the patches of color their kilties made in the elephant grass. I could see Suratan Singh, greasy and fat and panting in terror, crouching behind a slit of window, his eyes on the circle of doom that ringed him in. Lord! That old woman saw the drama in the scene; had me listening with nerves as well as ears. The grim Scotch soldiers closed in like a creeping death.

"And was the nabob all alone in that little mud house?" I asked.

"You ought to know," the old crone rasped. "He was alone in there with his priceless ruby!"

"How big was the ruby?" I wanted to know.

She glared at me as if I'd asked a silly question; then made a five-foot sweep with her twiglike hand. I understood. It was the biggest ruby in the world, no question about it. The old woman chattered something about the extreme beauty of said ruby, launched a spate of fantastic Oriental metaphors likening the ruby to a goddess and a star, uncorked a lot of terms I couldn't catch and ended by letting me understand that Suratan Singh had owned a roomful of treasures and that naturally the one he'd try to take with him in exile would be the best of the lot and a marvel beyond comprehension.

**THEN** she carried me back to the little mud house, darkness falling, the stalwart Highlanders with their shiny bayonets and death in their eyes getting ready for the final rush. All this the old woman saw as a shivering girl crouching behind a *peepul* tree on the rim of the village.

Believe me, it had made an impression. She described the white soldiers as giants of the most ferocious caste. I could almost feel sorry for the lone Hindu who waited, with his paunch heaving in fright, for the rush to come. But he didn't wait.

The old woman told me she didn't know how he'd got out. But suddenly something scooted past the *peepul* tree where she, the frightened girl, crouched hiding. And she saw in the dark gloom the figure of the Hindu nabob as he sneaked, unseen by the white soldiers, through the grass. Did he have his treasure with him? You bet he did. My story-teller told me she saw that, too. By the Oath of the Cow, Suratan Singh was not the one to leave his most valued possession behind. He was creeping along as silently as the fall of night from the East, and carrying the treasured ruby with him.

Then she croaked out that she'd left her post at the *peepul* tree and started after the fleeing prince. She'd had to move like anything to keep up with the fugitive, for he'd chosen a path that the devil himself would have hated to follow. Through thorn-brush and brier, across a snake-infested bog, deep into elephant grass.

As if he cared more for his treasure than his life, this Suratan Singh had become agile as the monkey god Hanaman, who'd trod a dangerous bridge of stones to carry a goddess from

Ceylon to the mainland. Old Suratan had traveled across a few stones, himself. The girl who followed him saw blood where his torn feet had stepped.

When she got to this point in her story, the old woman creaked to her feet. "But perhaps the white *sahib* is tired," she cackled. "Mayhap you wish to hear no more. Are you still interested?"

Interested! I was seeing a Hindu dash along through the brush, clutching a gem that twinkled rays of fire, a jewel beyond value and big as a house. You bet I was interested!

"Keep talking," I ordered, hoarse-voiced. "This Hindu with his treasure. Where did he go?"

A laugh crackled out of the woman's toothless mouth, and she pointed into the ravine from which I'd rescued her not half an hour before.

"He ran along the bottom of that gully," she wheezed. "If you desire it, we can follow his trail from there."

We followed his trail from there.

**THE WOMAN** found a path crawling to the ravine's bottom, and I followed as if I were mesmerized. I'm not too certain I wasn't. The legend of Suratan Singh had been percolating in my blood for a long time, and it only needed a little jolt to set me off. And this old woman's story was no little jolt.

She was handing me the key to a puzzle that had harried the wiliest of Asia's treasure-hunters for eighty-odd years, and I must have gone a little light-headed. For I forgot my mission for the museum, slung my rifle under arm and started after that gossiping hag.

That ruby must have mesmerized old Suratan, too. He surely picked himself one hell of a route. We thrashed down the ravine bottom, and the thorns began to stick like darts from my arms, legs, palms, and posterior. We advanced down a dried-up watercourse where the pebbles were sharp as knives.

The moonlight dropped shadows to betray my feet, and I stumbled like a drunkard. In half an hour I was gasping, sweat-wet, bleeding from a million scratches. But I was going to the spot where the great jewel lay. The ancient crone padded along in front of me, grimacing, grinning, beckoning—a rawhide marionette.

Quiet? This was the place where echoes came to die. Only the sound of stones set scampering by our heels, the occasional yelp of a jackal, the whisper of hot wind through leaves, disturbed that Asian stillness that casts a spell. Before I knew it the moon had gone. Some time later the stars winked out and a dash of flame leaped across the East.

Now we were burrowing into deep hills, and I could see the tops of tall cliffs stabbing skyward out of jungle green. Hot, chrome-yellow dawn gave promise of a scorching day, found me limping in rags through a bamboo grove, and brought a semblance of sanity to my addled brain.

"What a fool I am," I thought when I knelt beside a pool for a drink and sighted what had been my face written over with scratches, black with grime, bubbling sweat. I yelled at the woman: "How much farther?"

"Not far!" she answered, and the vision of a ruby that glowed like a planet seduced reason, and I plunged on after the witch. I've hit some mighty evil country in my day, but I never saw a stretch to equal the *terai* we crossed that morning. Never!

Thorns, briers, nettles weren't the half of it. Open ground was peppered with tiny stones, adze-sharp. There were bogs of mud like black glue. Jungles where the vines hung in loops from the palm trees and slapped at your eyes. Swamps clouded with malarial steam, seeping and stinking, breeding grounds for those little *krait* snakes that are deadly as bullets from a Lüger. And overhead a blazing, withering sun that hit like a fist on your neck.

**I TELL** you, the thought of that ruby was the only thing to keep me on my feet. Every time I'd start to grumble, every time I'd stop to rest, the old woman leading me would remind me of the story. As I fought up the trail she chattered.

She made me see that terrified, two-thirds-dead Hindu nabob humping along for dear life, carrying his ruby. She made me see the grim-faced white troopers hounding the fleeing Hindu's heels.

I could fathom the fright of that hounded wretch. After all, he wasn't just a pot-bellied native prince. He was a human being. How his mouth must have yawped with fear every time he heard the soldiers behind him. How his bones must have been racked.

I could appreciate that. My own bones were getting some racking. The heat on my back was roasting, too, and the sun hadn't been any less hot that July of 1857.

The crone was tough. You have to be tough to grow old in North India. And she was a native and used to those hills. I was not. I don't suppose Suratan Singh was, either. The old woman in front of me halted to throw a stick at a green snake.

"Suratan went through those trees," she pointed out. "I remember the banyan yonder. There was blood where he had walked. And all the time he carried his treasure, so."

She crooked her good arm and wiggled the bones making fingers for her hand, and I wondered if Suratan had run along holding his jewel in front of him, watching its fire-colored blaze, holding it there to keep courage. It must have taken something more than mere fear of death to shove the man over this plague-spot. The old woman said so, too.

"For the prince it was terrible," the hag croaked out. "The white giants were after him with gleaming knives at the ends of their guns. They wore boots. Suratan was bare of foot. He had no time to stop and rest the way they did. *Ahee!* He must run, run, run. He must fly to save his precious ruby. The white men followed like the evil spirits of Shaitan. Sometimes they were close. They would see him. They would shoot—"

*Bang!* This story was getting realistic as the devil. No sooner had the old hag uttered the word "shoot," than a gunshot smashed through the jungle. My helmet spun from my head with a hole drilled through its crown!

**MY NOSE-DIVE** for cover was a fast one, I can promise you. I didn't need a little bird to tell me what had happened. Those coolies of mine. That tall guide with the flower behind his ear. They'd overheard the crone's treasure-tale. They'd been awed at first, then talked it over among themselves. If the white *sahib* thought this ruby was worth finding, there must be something in it. There were rifles in my luggage. They'd armed themselves, and started after me.

In the bamboo grove I'd left a moment before, another gun cracked. A bullet whined past my ear to ricochet from a tree with a *ping*. I screamed at the old woman, telling her to duck; and then let fly a fusillade at the bamboos.

My own fire was answered by a lively hail of pellets that stung overhead and pruned a lot of orchid leaves. The whole ten of those coolies must have let fly. Here was a situation to tickle my scalp.

"We've got to get out of here!" I bawled at the old woman. "Where can we go?"

The gums worked in the hag's shrunken mouth. "We must follow the trail taken by Suratan," she snarled. "It is the only way of escape for you. You cannot go back from here."

"Get on, then!" I yelled; and we got. I had something besides the thought of a ruby to keep me moving now. You bet I had! I scrabbled after that old woman, tearing through the underbrush; and ten coolies, bent on stopping me, came after. Every half mile or so I'd stop to slip a load of cartridges into my Mannlicher rifle and spray bullets at the brush behind me. My pursuers would uncork a shot or two to let me know they were still there; and I'd gather my tired bones together and run some more.

Listen! All that blatant, furnace-hot afternoon and throughout the next hot night I plugged up that wilderness trail, led by that incredible witch-woman and followed by that blood-thirsty gang.

Maybe you think the sardonic aspect of the thing wasn't brought home to me! Here I was, following that trail broken by Suratan Singh. I'd changed places with the Hindu. He'd been hounded by a squad of Scotch Highlanders. I was dogged by a crowd of ruffian natives. Man, I was fit to be tied.

We gave the natives the slip about dawn, and just as the sun was stoking the sky for a second day of record heat I staggered into a forest of *mohors* where the mud was knee-deep and the temperature so stifling that the fetid air seemed to sizzle. The swampy forest-bottom smoked. The slime seemed to simmer for all the world like a caldron of pitch.

Perhaps you think that hundred-year-old hag was tuckered out? She was not. You could hear her hide squeaking as she rocked along, but I think she could have marched forever. Her nerves and feelings had been worn out long ago. I think her insides were sawdust. How can you tire out sawdust?

But my insides weren't sawdust, by a long shot. My eyes were baked marbles in my head. My tongue was a chunk of burned cake. My throat was a red string. I'd had nothing to eat save a few raw berries; nothing at all to drink for five hours. My hands and feet were swollen and cut, my neck blistered; the thorns stuck out of my hide like bristles on a porcupine. And any minute a lead slug might drone from behind to crack me in the spine or through the heart.

"Courage!" my tireless guide adjured. "Did not Suratan follow this very path? And remember: he carried his treasure."

Regardless of scorpions, I plopped myself down on a rotting log, and fanned what was left of my face with what was left of my helmet. I panted and winked sweat from my eyes and glared at the woman.

"To hell with Suratan and his treasure!" I snarled. "I can't take another damned step!"

"Those who follow you will find you here," she suggested cheeringly.

"I can't take another damned step!" I repeated.

Her wrinkled face cackled a chuckle, and she pointed a hooking thumb. "Five steps more will carry you out of these trees," she said. "The end of Suratan's trail is there."

I took those five steps on the bound. Then I stopped in my tracks with a yell.

**IN THIS** day and age of superlatives and airplanes, a thousand feet up sounds ordinary. But don't you believe it. Stand on the pavement in front of the Woolworth Building in New York and tilt your head. It doesn't shaft skyward a thousand feet, but it seems to climb up to the moon.

Then fancy my feelings when I slogged out of the trees and found myself standing on the edge of a grassy acre of ground backed by a cliff wall that shot to the clouds. Wow!

The *terai* jungle came to a dead stop in front of that wall. The ground made a thousand-foot leap at one jump and became the Himalaya Mountains.

A giant scimitar had hacked off the slope of the Himalayas to make room for more lowland beneath. Or else that cliff was a stone wall reared on the rim of the world. I stared up that wall, and the eyes swelled big in my head. My vision swam. Whew! That wall towered sheer, like the side of a building—one vast, blank sweep shooting up and up, smooth as glass, and stopping only when it touched the blue.

Feathery puffs of cloud clustered at the cliff-top. The early morning sunshine shafted across its bleak face. High in the air an eagle wheeled; so high it was small as a gnat. And that was only halfway up the incredible cliff. Say, it gave me the creeps.

I stood glaring up that mighty escarpment of stone, open-mouthed. You know the feeling it gives you to see something unexpected and vast. Awe and dizziness and a queer desire to yawn. Empathy, the psychologists call it. Right then I was suffering a double dose of empathy.

Then I remembered something, and I jumped about with a growl. It wouldn't do for me to stand yawping when the jungle behind me was hiding the advance of a thug-gang after my scalp.

"This is the end of the trail!" I yelled at the old woman. "Where is the treasure of Suratan? Where do we go from here?"

The rag, bone and hair-hank got a finger into the air. "Up!"

"*Up!*" I snarled. "What the devil do you mean?"

"It is the only way you can go," she cackled. "The hill-men come along the trail back there. It was even so with Suratan, who ran from the white giants with the knives."

Her words went through my brain like a hot wire. I saw what I'd done. I'd chased up the bottom of a valley and was caught at its end like a cat at the end of a blind alley. Trapped as nicely as you please. I was mad, I can tell you. I gave that witch a glance that should have knocked off her head.

"You old fool!" I squalled, thinking of the ten coolie gunmen cutting off my escape. "You've got us caught now! Caught like rats!" The sweat stood out on my forehead. "Any minute those jackals will pop out of these trees. Ten to one. You—"

She gestured. "It was even so with Suratan. Any minute the white tigers would be out of the trees. Only three of them trailed him; but he had no gun. Look! One of the white soldiers did come out of the trees." She pointed at the moss under her feet.

Hot-eyed I stared. There, embedded in the ground, rotted to dust, lay the stock of a musket and the crumbling-remains of a rusted gunbarrel.

"See!" croaked the crone. "The white soldier reached here. But he did not catch Suratan. Suratan went *up!*"

She pointed again at that sheer shot of cliff.

"You mean," I shouted, "that Suratan climbed that wall?"

"To the top," she growled, wagging her head. "And you must climb it, too, if you would find the treasure of Suratan and escape your enemies. Remember, *sahib,* how tired he was. Remember, he carried his treasured ruby with him. But the white soldiers were close behind. He climbed. Look!" She slipped past me and went to the base of the cliff. "See—there are steps. Cut in the stone by the gods."

**NOT TILL** then did I notice a succession of little niches gouged out of the stone and laddering a straight line up that cliff-side. Mere hand-holds, they were, affording about as much grip for fingers and toes as would bricks jutting three inches from the face of a smooth brick wall. Lord alone knows how those niches had been made. Perhaps by Dravidian priests lowered from the cliff-top in rope slings with chisel and maul to peck out the most horrible stairway in the universe.

Those niches were so small you could not see them forty feet above ground unless you looked hard. As for climbing by them—no wonder the thousand and one treasure-hunters who'd sought Suratan hadn't come to the end of his trail.

"You say he went up this cliff!" I whispered. I had to whisper from the very thought of it.

"He climbed the steps," answered the old woman, "carrying his treasured ruby. So." She made a pantomime I couldn't understand. "And he was not fifty hands high on the wall before the white soldier ran from the trees and saw him. I was over there, hiding in the rhododendron, and I saw it all. The white giant lifted his gun and started to shoot. Suratan kept climbing. The bullets struck the wall near his hands. I could see the chips fly from the stone where they struck. Think!"

I thought of it, and it made the sweat wash down into my mouth. That wretch of a Hindu scrambling up the face of that cliff, clinging to a ladder no fireman or human fly would dare to look at. The Scotch Highlander darting from the jungle, standing on the very fan of ground where I now stood, pot-shooting at that fat and gasping Hindu crawling up the wall.

It made my jaw rattle. The old crone told how the Scotchman fired again and again. Don't blame that soldier. He'd gone through hell to catch this Hindu prince. Those days of the Mutiny were terrible days. Neither side would give quarter.

"The white giant's weapon spoke many times, but Suratan climbed on. At last the white man fell exhausted and sick. He had taken the fever as he crossed the *terai* after Suratan, and from where I hid I could see death in his eye. But he lay there on the ground and his gun continued to speak. *Ahee!*"

What a monumental struggle that was! The dying Scot fighting with his last breath. That bedeviled Hindu working a miracle to save himself—and his treasure, as the old woman kept repeating. Lordy!

I could see that Scotch soldier with fever-madness in his eye; see that Hindu's figure growing smaller and smaller as it scaled that fearful height. The Scotty lay on the ground and sniped. He wasn't going to let that nabob escape. He'd seen white women butchered by these Hindus. He wanted with all the furious and terrible will of the Scot to work a just retribution.

"But Suratan reached the top!" the woman chanted. "And he lies there with his treasure to this day. I know. And if the white *sahib* would find this place where Suratan lies, if the white *sahib* would save his own life, he must climb as Suratan climbed before him."

I was trembling in every limb. "I can't!" I groaned. "I can't!" And suddenly I was at that terrible wall, starting up hand over hand.

**IN NEW YORK** during the war I saw a man go up the front of a skyscraper to advertise Liberty Bonds. He'd stop every ten feet or so, look down, yell his jeremiad at the crowd, and the crowd would roar. My start up that dizzy cliff was somewhat similar. I could just get my fingers into those niches and kick for a toe-hold. Then with a terrific effort of will I could worm one toe into the next niche up, fling a hand to catch at another of those shallow notchings in the wall-face, and, hugging the stone, yank myself another lap skyward. Then, with the breath steaming from my clenched teeth, the sweat leaking into my eyes, I'd glance down and yell—I don't know why.

There was no crowd below to spur me on—at first. There was

only that old *mihtrani* hag. Every time I'd look down in terror she'd point at the sky and remind me that Suratan had made the grade. Then she'd laugh.

That laugh! It rivaled the cackle of a peacock; but it burned into my aching head as the call of Circe must have scorched the ears of the luckless Greek sailors. It made me bite my lips and close my eyes and think of the fabulous fortune at cliff-top and *climb*. It moved me up that wall.

Can you see that picture of me clinging to that shot of blank stone? Inching my way to its top like a fly on a windowpane—but wearing no gauze wings on which to float away should my fingers miss the clutch or my foot make a slip. Lordy! My feet *did* slip. A hundred times. Then I'd hang by bleeding finger-tips and kick till I'd find the notch. Then I'd plaster myself against that wall and wait trembling while the sweat simmered out of my pores.

I was a hundred feet in the air when I noticed tiny gougings from the stone near my hand-niches. Wow! Those were the places the Scotch soldier's bullets had struck as he tried to bring down the fat Hindu. I began to appreciate that Hindu nabob. I was inspired to achieve a height of two hundred feet. Thank God no one was sniping at me.

*Spang!* I'd thought of the devil; now I heard his sweet voice. The gunfire sounded like a hammer-tap below me, and splinters flew from the wall above. I made the mistake of looking down. In the clearing below the old woman was not to be seen. But black heads and brown shoulders were there, and I caught the bright sheen of gun-metal. The metal spat flame as half a dozen shots barked, and the splinters scattered down on my sweat-plastered hair.

I went up that wall all right, then. Believe you me, that was life's darkest hour. I clawed and kicked and yanked myself up. My arms wanted to tear from their shoulder-sockets. My hands and knees were raw as open wounds. My throat knotted in my neck. My spine was an icicle.

Every inch of the climb was contested by steel slugs that smacked all around me like buckshot. The bullets struck with a *whing* and ricocheted with a whistle. Chips of stone cut at my cheeks. One shot ripped a rag from my sleeve, and I couldn't help glancing at that piece of cloth circling down and down and down....

I climbed. Brain, heart, and soul went dead. My nerves expired. I was an automatic thing, moving by reflexes. A thing that clawed for a hand-hold, kicked for a foothold, battled against the law of gravity, and hauled itself upward toward the sky. The bullets stung around me, but I didn't care. Lord knows why I hung on and kept going.

That cliff was high! Higher than the Woolworth Building. The wall below me sped downward like the wall of an elevator shaft. The men on the ground below were ants. The air in which I was suspended was thin. I was five hundred feet above ground, ready to plunge into eternity, unable to let go. It makes me sick to think about it. It turns my stomach to this day.

**THE THEOLOGIANS** are wrong. I know. The way to hell is not down; it is up. It goes up to a height even bullets can scarcely attain, and the top of this dizzy road overhangs so that the creature who reaches that awful peak must clutch and claw and kick himself over a cornice of stone before he can stand on his feet beneath the clouds.

You understand? The top of that cliff bulged like a forehead, and I had to climb up over this bulge by means of those shallow niches in the solid rock. I brayed when I saw that bulge. Perhaps I prayed.

At any rate, I seem to have rounded the thing, somehow. Like a bug rounding the under side of an orange, I imagine. I know Newton would never have believed his law if he'd seen me do it—had he seen me clawing and hanging and scraping and dragging my flagellated, nerveless carcass up over that lofty cliff-rim.

I was over! I'd reached the top! I was lying horizontal on my belly, scrabbling on a flat surface, fainting, mouthing, wriggling lizard-like to get away from the edge of that awful precipice. I was spraddling on a bald plateau that sloped away under the clouds and fell with a gentle declivity to the edge of a dark green forest. I clutched at the ground to keep from falling off that level stretch!

Somewhere distant a temple bell was tolling. There would be a town—a road—people! I laughed, and the sound of my voice was that of a saw on dull wood, raspy in the thin clear air.

Then I was stiff on my hands and knees, staring. Staring wide-eyed at a skeleton of white bones that lay on the patch of rock before me. There on the rim of that cliff lay those bones, and I crawled to them with my tongue out. That skeleton lay staring at the sky, grinning in the same sunshine that found a glint of metal under its breastbone. My eyes hung out of my head. Sticking there in the framework of that skeleton's ribs was a long, thin, double-edged knife. I whispered: "Suratan Singh!"

Then I yelped. Beside this first frame of bones lay another, a smaller skeleton! You understand? A second skeleton!

It sprawled, face down on the rock, and I saw with astonishment that the wrist-bones of its left arm were encircled by a little silver bracelet! Then I saw something else—something that dropped me to my face with a sob. The base of this second skeleton's skull was punctured by a small round hole; and the skeleton was that of a woman!

**BRADSHAW** was pounding his fist on his knee, and his voice had begun to shake.

"You get it, man? You see it? There were two skeletons up there! Two! Suratan Singh had carried a woman with him when he left his little mud hut to make his get-away from the British. All the way through that awful *terai* he'd carried her!

"Think of that fat, heathen Hindu doing that! The old hag who led me over his trail had tried to explain that. But her unfamiliar dialect and her flowery metaphors had gone over my head. I hadn't comprehended her gestures.

"The Hindu, though, chased by those Highlanders, had carried a girl in his arms all the way to that cliff. Then, think! He'd slung her on his back somehow and carried her up that horrible precipice wall! Lordy! While the lone soldier who'd managed to trail him stood below and blazed away with his rifle.

"That soldier was out of his head from fever and sun, but his bullets hit close. Too close. One of them struck that girl in the back of her head. The poor devil of a Hindu kept climbing; he didn't know she was dead. Torn to pieces by the jungle, tired enough to die, he climbed that awful wall with a girl on his back; reached the top.

"Can you see that poor devil, then? Just ahead lay the way to freedom—a forest, a road—the road I took to reach Nani Tal. All the way to Nani Tal I thought of that Hindu, and I was sick. He'd beaten his way up that wall, only to find the girl dead when he gained the top. I could see him bending over that poor slain creature, with all the hell of the universe in his eyes. Then he pointed his knife at his heart—"

The naturalist mopped at his face. His cheeks were drawn, gray in the evening dusk. Presently he resumed the narrative.

"That's the point of my story, man! Suratan Singh hadn't wrought that frightful road of escape for the saving of any mere gem. He'd forged the bravest gesture in the world, and he'd done it for love. Far as I'm concerned, he's expiated all the sins of India's benighted race; bought honor for all the men of the world! You'd know, if you'd scaled that precipice. If India still breeds her sons like that, she'll never sit back to be ruled."

"But the treasure!" I demanded stupidly. "The famous ruby—?"

Bradshaw shook his head. "There's no word for 'the' in the Hindustani language, or the written Hindee. That is what fooled the legend-makers who read Suratan's note to his brother. That's what misled me in the old crone's description of Suratan's flight. In each case no mention was made of *a* treasure or *the* gem. There are no articles in Hindustani, remember. Suratan had written: 'I carry with me my most precious treasure—my most precious ruby.' We who hunted him supplied the 'a' and 'the.' In this case we were mistaken. Look."

The naturalist groped, and drew from his pocket a little hoop of silver. "That's the bracelet I found on her wrist."

He handed the bracelet to me. On the under side of the band were engraved these Hindee characters:

"The word is *la'l*, isn't it?" I said wonderingly. "Why, that means—"

"That's right," Bradshaw sighed. "Her name—Ruby."

# THE PHANTOM BUDDHA

*Said the yellow monk with a smile wan:*
*"Hast thou seen the Buddha of Ban Panan?"*
*"There's no such thing to be seen," I cried*
*And, lo! the phantom was at my side!*
*—Bradshaw's "Ballads of the East"*

CURSING FRANTICALLY, CLAWING at the tangling
vines, the man broke from the thicket, plunged across the bog
and raced up the shadowy trail. An enormous dollar-round
moon, wheeling into the indigo sky behind him, shed a curious,
ethereal glow to pick out the ashen pallor of his face. Back in
the thicket he had lost his sun helmet. His yellow hair tossed
damply as he ran. Globes of sweat, like drops of melting wax,
leaked down his panting cheeks. The darkness was oppressive
with heat, but the runner was not perspiring from warmth. He
was sweating with fear. Terror. Terror drove the drops wiggling
down his face and propelled his muddied heels down the night-
hung path.

The blood-orange moon wheeled behind a smoky screen of
clouds, and the runner halted for a moment in green darkness.
Halted, sighed and listened. From the gully hedged by the
pandanus thickets rose a turbulent, buzzing murmur. The drone
of many excited voices; the clamor of milling, excited men. The
drone rose to high pitch, moaned down to an echo; rose and
fell like the voices of a hundred ministers intoning prayers on
a slumberous afternoon.

The runner's youthful face went candle-color. His scared eyes sought the shadows in his path. A trembly hand found weighty blue steel at his hip. The feel of cold metal in his fist loaned confidence to his legs. Coughing for breath, he immersed himself in the whispering glooms of the crooked trail, and scampered into the sceneless dark.

Behind him the valley droned its weird, excited chant. The moon crept clear of the clouds and shed its occult light to make of those gloom-veiled jungle bottoms a kobold world.

**THE TINTED** twilight had melted away behind the kaladangs on the hill, and the suffocation that had threatened the afternoon seemed imminent. Heat mists roved the lime groves crowding the naturalist's bungalow. The humid dark perspired. Even the monkeys, prepared to screech their evening roundelay on the compound fence, were stifled to a small-voiced chattering. The jungle beyond the fence was smothered in tropic night; pitch-black, torpid, still.

Despite the enervating nightfall, an animated discussion engaged those on the bungalow verandah. Bradshaw, the gaunt Kelantan naturalist, was there, and Schneider, the beery Dutchman from Islamahad, and McInerny, the engineer come to boss the running of steel up to the tin mines behind the mountain.

"You can't tell me anything," McInerny was announcing in a strident tone. The declaration was in keeping with his bulldog jaw, wiry red hair and stubborn blue eyes that tossed back glints of lamp light. A man who stood six-feet-four and had killed with a punch the China Coaster who had knifed that baleful Z-shaped scar across his temple, could afford to be assertive. "You can't tell me anything about this hoodoo voodoo rot. Maybe you don't know it, but that's just the reason I was sent out here from Calcutta to run this job. To lay a few ghosts. The company knows I'm one engineer who don't scare easy. This Orient witchery stuff never bothered me. I was from Missouri when I first came East, an' I'm still from there. Guess I've lived in th' Orient long enough by now to know this Asia mystery-atmosphere stuff is junk cooked up by the thriller books. Oh, I've seen a couple snake charmers an' contortionists worth lookin at, yes. But you'd see better stuff back on Broadway. As for these mango tricks, an' throwin' ropes up to heaven, an' buryin' alive for three weeks stunts, I ain't never seen one of 'em. An' I been six years in India." He grunted scornfully. "I claim this Asia stuff is all damned nonsense. I'm an Irishman who don't see ghosts. I've never seen any Oriental charms an' I don't believe in anything unless I see it with my own eyes. I'll believe anything I can see. Seeing," he concluded sententiously, "is believin'. I'll *believe* what I *see*."

Bradshaw stared at the scarlet coal in the kalabash he insisted on smoking; then said tolerantly: "That's all right, Mr. McInerny. But I only claim there's a lot of weirdness floating around the world, and the East seems more tuned to catch it. Just to watch the sun roll down out here is a psychic, uncanny business for me. I don't blame these jungle natives for having imaginations. Look at that darkness out there. It's the very essence of black, eh? And that big red moon coming up back of the hill. Gets under *my* skin, I can tell you.

"Listen. I've seen all those illusions you just mentioned never having witnessed. A leprous old Hindu with halitosis something awful worked that mango trick right under my nose up in Allahabad. I've seen a Punjabi yogi throw a rope up to the stars. And in Siam I saw a priest buried three weeks ten hours under sand. Just clever tricks, that's all. The last is just a matter of expert nerve control and getting oxygen out of the sand. But there are other Oriental stunts like hypnotism—that sort of thing—not easily laughed off. These Asians can *feel*. I've come to this conclusion. Believe what you *can't* see, an' be damned skeptical of what you *see!*"

The big engineer grunted derisively as he reached for the gin and bitters. "I'll stick to my point. I'll believe what I see. I don't go in for heavy imagination. Guess I got the fighting end of my Irish blood, with the superstition left out." He drank with a practised gulp. "I'm havin' enough trouble with this Oriental superstition hokum. That's why I'm out here now. Carter, the young Boston kid we had runnin' th' job, ain't been able to handle th' coolies. They're all hopped up on this mystery stuff; see a witch behind every tree in th' jungle. Too busy spotting spooks to lay track. Carter is all nerves, too. Good enough engineer but can't buffalo down this Oriental bunko. He'd been havin' plenty trouble, so the company sent me out to get things moving faster. We got to get down so much steel a week or we lose our contract."

Schneider panted: "So you haff come to lay ghosts as well as track, McInerny? You railroaders are like that. Mathematical men with muscles, *ja*. And you haff the muscles. You are not afraid of ghosts and do not believe in them, eh?"

The Irishman sneered. "What's the use of bein' childish. Take these coolies workin' our job. They're all nerves about this legend sayin' a Buddha is goin' to walk th' Ban Panan cliff one of these nights. Our camp's right by there, an' th' steel goes right under th' hill. All I can do to get them damned yellow punks to work the job."

**"IT'S THE** old phantom Buddha legend you hear in all these lotus-flower countries," Bradshaw explained to his fat friend. "The ancient Buddhasatva superstition. Story has it that Gautama, himself, once walked up that Ban Panan trail along the cliff wall. Now the natives believe that every full moon

Buddha—or his ghost—strolls up that trail again, looking for converts to follow him. Every native in these jungles claims he's seen the phantom, too."

"It's a troublesome lot of hooey," McInerny growled sourly. "Th' coolies are popeyed about it. Most of th' beggars are Buddhists. Few days ago one of these skinny, one-eyed monk devils with a shaved head an' beggin' bowl turned up in camp. Stuffed the rice-eaters full of that phantom yarn, sayin' the Buddha would show up almost any time now. Stirred 'em up to beat hell, an' got under Carter's skin, it seems. The Boston kid was all eyes when he told me about it. I asked him if he believed such bloody foolishness, an' he said you couldn't tell about the Orient. Say! I told him I could handle that tommyrot. An' if that one-eyed nut showed up in camp to lecture th' coolies again, I'd hang a fist on his yella jaw he wouldn't forget. That track's got to go down fast, an' no fool ghost nonsense is gonna stop it. We been fighting the Curtis Construction Ltd. outfit. You know that big Singapore crowd. If we lose th' contract, they grab th' job."

"That Curtis crowd iss a hard bunch," Schneider commented. "A rich company. *Ja,* I know them. They own everything from Singapore to Saigon. Mines, plantations, steamboats. They are the ones who haff built that big hotel and moving picture in Bangkok. Modern business. Old Curtis is a skinflint, that is so. One tough outfit, I should say."

"Yeh." The Irishman stood to his six-four, grinning self-confidence. Lantern glow gleamed in his eyes, and he touched the Z-shaped scar on his temple with a knotty fist, brushing away sweat. "But I'm tough as hell, myself. Soon as that Boston kid goes, an' I have full run of th' job, I'll show that Curtis gang. Th' East don't get under *my* skin to kid me into slowin' up no job. We're way behind on th' track, an' any more delay may lose us th' contract, but you guys leave it to me."

"Well," sighed the naturalist, "we hope you make out all right. Schneider and I have some small holdings in your company, and a lot of dislike for the Curtis bunch. They beat the devil out of any region they once get into. Goes hard with a few poor collectors like us. And thanks a lot for dropping in to get acquainted."

"Yeh. Sure. I'm th' guy for th' job, don't worry." The engineer pointed a thumb at the jungle where a crimson shoulder of moon was topping the fringe of foliage. "You know where th' camp is, about five miles up that trail. Drop up any time. Yeh. Thanks. I will have another *stengah* if you don't mind. I—"

**A SHRILL**, affrighted cry whipped out of the mohor grove on the edge the jungle. The men on the bungalow verandah jumped; peered. The next moment a shadow bounded from the trees, flickered through the gate and came sprinting across the compound. "Hey!" screeched the oncoming apparition. "Hey! Help!"

"Damn!" exploded McInerny. "It's Carter!"

Bradshaw and the Dutchman swore as they lowered their hastily-drawn automatics. The shadow became a lean figure, with face a pale, sweat-drenched oval; pounded doggedly on exhausted boots up to the verandah step. Standing with the moon glow on his white face, Carter exhaled a flurried rush of frightened words. The Irishman got a fist on his companion engineer's quaking arm.

"Stop yowling," he snapped angrily. "What's after you, kid? What the devil is wrong with you, now?"

"Nothing after me!" The boy gasped. "But—but I *saw* it! Saw it all, I tell you. The one-eyed monk said it would come. Tonight. He—he got the coolies together right under the cliff. They prayed. And then—then just as the moon came up—the monk waved a hand. And there on the trail—it appeared. The coolies went mad. It vanished—but—but the monk said it would come again. I saw it, too. It was there—and—you could see right through it. Walking up the trail. In a faint glow of light. There— there it was. The phantom Buddha!"

**SINGLE** file, the little column picked a path through the jungle, wading over inky bogs that were sheer treachery in the dark, kicking along creeper-tangled trails, clawing through lush groves of vine-matted palm and fungi-laden tapang. Save for the red, round moon dodging from cloud to cloud, there was no light. Bradshaw's electric torch had burned out, and the Irishman had tripped over a rotted log to smash the lantern he carried.

McInerny stalked in the lead with the tall naturalist. Schneider and the young engineer brought up a reluctant rear. McInerny's continual denouncements of the whole business as a piece of bloody rot had by no means relieved the stung nerves of Carter.

"We'll go back up to that camp with you and have a look, McInerny," Bradshaw had insisted. "Schneider and I. That boy is all shot to pieces about something, and I know these Malays well enough to realize what a riot can get under way if they once get hysterical about their superstitions. May be real trouble fomenting up there. This Carter lad must have really seen something to upset him this way."

"He's a damned fool," the big engineer had protested. "I guessed it when I met him three days ago. Now I know it. I got no patience with a bird who sees ghosts. But if that one-eyed hellion is rioting the coolies again, I'd better hop back to camp. Somebody's goin' to get in hot water about this. May be a little scrap, but I'll have those yella fat heads layin' track or I ain't Irish. You an' th' Dutchman can come along if you want. But I could handle it alone. Young Carter is a bigger fool than I thought he was. I wager he didn't see nothing at all."

"But I did see it!" Carter kept insisting. "There was that blank wall of cliff. Just as the moon came clear it appeared. God! It took the knees right out from under me. And those Malays went mad. It was there, all right. Walking up the path, in a queer white light—"

The Dutchman was willing to believe. Jungles at night wore on his nerves, and he made no bones about the fact. "I don't like this business," he complained, as he panted along. "I don't

like it a little bit. *Ach!* I am no giant with red hair to laugh at
the Orient. I am fat and always nervous in dark rooms. Shades
of Wilhelm der Zweite! I would rather be back in my hotel
with my meerschaum!"

"Uneasy, myself," the naturalist admitted, when his torch
flickered down. "That fat moon gives me the jumps. I'm beginning to feel as if there were specters on every hand. Whew! Be
glad when we come into open air once more—"

But McInerny could only curse as his feet slogged through
muck, and snarl at Carter to shut his silly mouth. The big Irishman shoved ahead, angrily defiant of nights and jungles. His
ponderous automatic glinted in his big fist as he floundered
along, and he raged with bull-like fury when progress was
slowed by a mucky fen alive with unseen snakes and chorusing
frogs.

"Of all the infernal rot!" he protested, halting to let the others
catch up. "I never seen th' like of it. Four grown men rushing
like hell to catch a fake ghost and kill a bugaboo. Carter, will
you cut out that wailing about seein' it! If anythin' gets on my
nerves it will be that. There. Thank God th' moon's comin' clear
an' we can see to make better time. Let's go, you guys. I want
to catch that yella monk fake an' sock his other eye out for him!"

Now the trail wound out of the swamp to cross a field of
serried elephant grass, white mists clung over the grass, and the
four men became wraiths. The field covered, their path led into
a forest of lofty sappans; then abruptly coiled out of the trees
to a glade cramped with pandanus. Carter dodged to the fore,
and held up a hand. His face was wry and ashen as he pointed
a finger at the trees ahead.

"The gully lies right back of that grove. You can see the top
of that Ban Panan cliff from here. See? The Malays are jammed
in th' gully, there. Right under the cliff. You can hear 'em, now.
Listen!"

They listened. Borne low on the torpid breeze drifted the
echoy murmur of many voices. They stared at the roof of cliff,

white behind the fringing trees. The voices rose and fell in the murky quiet. Schneider muttered a quaint Dutch oath. Bradshaw admitted a possibility of ghostly doings. McInerny hitched his weighty shoulders, and growled:

"Well, come on. I'm goin' to bust up this spiritual meeting!"

Leering, he plunged into the pandanus grove. Carter, Schneider and Bradshaw followed. The naturalist stole a look at his companions. Carter seemed to be regaining something of courage, but his eyes were uneasy under a matted sheaf of hair. The Dutchman's face was dripping.

"McInerny's right," the naturalist growled. "This is a lot of foolishness. Come on, fellows. Let's see what's bothering the coolies."

Creeping through the trees, close on the Irishman's heels, the naturalist gained a rise of ground thick with concealing underbrush. Then he was crouching in his tracks, forgetful of the big engineer at his side. In spite of himself, Bradshaw felt a little battalion of prickles go marching down his spine. The scene before his startled eyes might have been a painting on canvas. A painting by Gustave Dore. Portraying a nook in hell.

**THE KNOLL,** screened with undergrowth, overlooked a gully scooped bowl-like out of the hills. On three sides of this natural amphitheatre reared walls of whispery, black jungle foliage. The far side was faced by a shot of sheer cliff; a limestone curtain making a backdrop to a sandy stage. Crowding this fan of sand in the shadow of the cliff, a hundred Malay coolies knelt as if at prayer. Thick-wigged heads bobbed and ducked. Shoulders, that gleamed like burnished metal in the algid moonray, bowed in unison as yellow foreheads touched the ground. Skinny arms shot skyward as the salaaming heads came up, and a hundred voices chanted weird ritual that poured into the half-dusk a ululation.

On the fan of sand under the cliff wall stood the monk. Here was a truth stranger than any figment of imagination. The creature was a skeleton in a tattered canary-yellow *sarong*. His face was a mask pinned to his skull by that lone eye that shone like a coal in its unblinking sheath. His shaven crown glistened in the moonlight like an inverted brass tureen. Every time those Malays salaamed in prayer, that monk would fling a hand that was a twig up at the moon, and his toothless mouth would twist out a monotone that made those bobbing coolies twitch like dummies on a string. That yellow ancient was a necromancer, all right. He would chant and those coolies would chant. He would groan and every Malay there would groan with him. There was a wizard something in that lone-eyed skeleton's voice that made Bradshaw, the naturalist, want to groan and chant and plank his forehead on the ground, too.

"Lordy!" the naturalist managed. "I never saw anything like that before. I say. If there wasn't a donkey engine and a pile of rails and ties under that tall mohor down there, I wouldn't know the thing was real. Wow! Listen to that skinny monk's voice—"

The others were listening. Carter and the corpulent Dutchman were squatting like images. Strange, wide-eyed images that could perspire diamonds. Bradshaw could not see McInerny's face. But the Irishman's shoulders looming large in front of him were motionless as cut stone. Suddenly the big engineer demanded thickly: "What's that monk telling them? What's he say?"

"He told them Gautama the Buddha would appear any moment," Bradshaw whispered. He pointed to indicate a thin, gray, sigmoid line crawling up the smooth face of the cliff. "The monk says Buddha will walk that trail you see there. He claims Buddha will come out of Karma—I didn't just catch that—and appear, to lead sinners to the Eight-fold Trail for heaven. If they believe when they see the Gautama, and follow after the monk, their souls will be saved. Good Lord—"

"Look!" McInerny was on his feet. His voice became a squawk. "Look, there! By God! On that trail—"

The moon, turned to the color of cheese as it neared its zenith, had swung from the clasp of a gray cloud bank; and its unadulterated, brightest ray played full on the improbable gully of Ban Panan. Master of ceremonies, the bone-and-skin monk stood with stick-like arms upraised. The mob of coolies yelled and bobbed like a pack of maniacs. All could see that uncanny, mauve-tinted, luminous circle glowing on the bald face of the limestone cliff. A spot of light that might have been cast by the moon. And there, framed in the eerie glow, appeared a misty, shadowy living figure that seemed to stride along, the thread of trail, raising an arm and bowing its head as it moved.

The yellow monk intoned a singsong chant. The Malays howled. The moon edged behind the smoky, green clouds. The glow on the cliff face and the haloed wraith vanished. *"Om ma-ni pad-me! Hung!"* chanted the monk. *"Om ma-ni pad-me! Hung!"* moaned the Malays. "O, the jewel! O, the jewel in the lotus! Amen!"

Bradshaw, the naturalist, tried to close his yawping mouth, but he couldn't force it. That figure on the cliff trail! It had been alive and moving. And, fearfully enough, *transparent!* The naturalist fought to drag his eyes from the gully and snatch a glance at his companions. Schneider and the younger engineer were mummies in chalk. McInerny, the big Irishman, was paralysed in a half crouch. His face was obscure under the shadow of his sun helmet; but his hands were limp at his sides, and Bradshaw noticed he had let fall his automatic.

"O, the jewel! O, the jewel in the lotus!" wailed the coolies. The monk fired a fist towards the thinly-screened moon, and harangued. His voice was a sonorous prayer that strung tense wires through the half-gloom. His single eye was a star. He held that crowd of coolies in the palm of his hand, and worked them into hysteria with the wizardry of his toothless mouth. The jungle night was alive with nerves. McInerny heeled about, and got a clutch on Bradshaw's sleeve. "What's the monk saying now? What's he telling them now?"

"He's telling them to follow him. He will lead them to the truth, to the light, to Nirvana. The Buddha will appear for the last time, calling for converts. All who see must come. And—"

Bradshaw stiffened. "Listen to that! He's—he's telling them to turn from their oppressors! To destroy the work they have done for the white Christian. By God—"

*"Ach du lieber Gott im Himmel!"* Schneider croaked. "There it is again. Once more. The Buddha—"

"On the cliff trail!" squeaked McInerny.

"On the cliff!" shouted Carter. "But look! Those Malays!" The young engineer was dancing up and down. He was not watching the moving wraith that had reappeared as the moonlight washed down the cliff. He was pointing at the coolies who milled and swarmed across the newly-laid roadbed bifurcating the gully. "They're tearing up the steel—"

It was Bradshaw who flung into action. "You're right, kid," he shouted. "Quick! I—I've got this figured, now. Hey! Quick, men. Don't let those maniacs wreck the job! McInerny! You and Schneider get to the other end of the gully! Fast! Guns out! Carter! Can you hold this end? Good boy! Get that monk! Get that yellow monk! Keep the Malays back to the cliff! Don't let 'em move till I get back! Hold 'em boys! I'm going to smash this phantom business—"

McInerny had already gone. Carter and the Dutchman rushed to obey Bradshaw's commands. Cursing to himself, the naturalist thrashed off through the trees. His automatic nested in his fist, and the queerest of smiles set sternly on his mouth.

**IT WAS** the big mohor that looked across the amphitheatre of the gully towards the cliff wall. To Bradshaw it seemed a year that he fought his way through the jungle fencing in the glade. But at last, after an age of tearing through briar, mud and vine, he found the lofty tree a few rods ahead of him. From his present position he could not see the gully, but he could hear the hysterical racketing of the Malays, and he wanted to get to that tree before any chance shooting would commence.

Yes, he had guessed it! He cursed under his breath. There was that droning noise faint above the roar of milling men. He charged forward, and gained the base of the tree. The foliage above him was a black screen, but he could hear that low droning clearly, now. He waited, panting. The moonlight flickered out and the droning ceased. Bradshaw grinned and hunched low in the briar. A queer, dark shadow came wraithlike, with the agility of a spider, down the black trunk of the mohor. Bradshaw charged from the brush, stabbing out hard with the muzzle of his gun.

There was the shock of metal against flesh, a brief flurry of white fists, soft oaths, the stamp of feet. The shape that had slithered down the tree took form as a man. A queer steel box dropped from the man's arms as he flung to meet Bradshaw's attack. But the naturalist saw it, and yelled as he pounded at his adversary.

"Don't try to hide it, you fool! I got you! With the goods, too. Stick 'em up, or I'll drill you full of holes—"

Pale fists drove into Bradshaw's face, knocked aside the gun. They wrestled fiercely, tripping on roots. Bradshaw struck hard, his knuckles hit bone with a smart crack, and a dark head banged savagely against the tree trunk. Another second, and the automatic nested again in Bradshaw's fist, the muzzle fixed on a swollen, beaten eye.

"Coming now?" Bradshaw's voice was harsh. The dark head nodded. "Then march!" The man marched, hands reaching high. Bradshaw held the automatic close, and the man marched out of the thicket and into the gully. Here was an odd scene. A hundred Malay coolies jammed together in a chattery crowd, backed against the cliff that frowned skyward against a dim, lurking moon. A tall lad with hay-colored hair and a damp face holding back one fringe of the crowd with a waving automatic. A fat, gasping Dutchman commanding the other edge of the mob with ready oaths and a revolver. The Dutchman and the tall lad yelled.

"Curtis!" the young engineer shouted out. "Curtis of Singapore!"

*"Herr Gott!"* Schneider panted. "It iss the old crook, himself. Whiskers and all!"

"Where's McInerny?" Bradshaw booted his captive to the fore. "He'd recognize the old grafter, too."

Schneider waved a fat hand. "You did not see? It was just as you were giving orders that McInerny charged down into the mob. I guess maybe he was fighting mad. The last I saw of him he was chasing that one-eyed monk. Chased him off into the jungle, running like a cat. *Ja—*"

"And now Curtis can explain!" Bradshaw snarled. "You can tell those fool Malays all about it. Tell 'em how you hoaxed that phantom to make 'em riot. Tell 'em how you played up that monk an' then hid yourself in that tree. Tell 'em how you made the ghost appear when the moon was shining, so's the moon-light would wipe out the ray from your machine. Go ahead, Curtis. I'll go back to that tree and fetch it. I'll go back there and get your little *movie picture machine—*"

**IT WAS** some weeks later on Bradshaw's bungalow verandah. Evening. Shadows that that should have been cool gathering quietly under the limes. The jungle beyond the compound fence whispering softly in the tinted dusk. Bradshaw talking to Fenway, the trader from down river, and Carter, the young engineer who had run steel to the mines beyond the mountain.

Bradshaw was concluding a story for Fenway, who hadn't heard the details. Staring at the coal in his kalabash, the natu-ralist sighed. "I confess when I saw that wraith on the stone cliff I could have broken an artery. You know how that Ban Panan valley drips atmosphere. Lord! It was a mighty swell illusion, I tell you. The cliff made a perfect screen for the picture, and the moonlight killed the ray from the machine. It was the dandiest ghost a chap could hope to see. But listen. One thing was off the books. My eye spotted something the rest of the mob was too scared to notice. That ghost wore a hood over its head, but I caught a glimpse of a bearded face. All of a sudden, I knew. That was a snapshot of Curtis. Can you beat it! It was pretty hazy and indistinct, but I'd know that old bounder's face in a fog. Curtis, it was. Curtis all dressed up and had himself filmed on one of those little movie cameras. Curtis in the role of a Buddha—"The naturalist laughed shortly behind his pipe-smoke.

"But the queerest thing of all," Carter commented, "was the disappearance of McInerny. You know, he went chasing after that yellow monk like a bat out of hell. Last we saw of him he was after that rice-eater like a cat after a mouse, ripping into the jungle. And the pair of them just vanished. We hunted. We hunted like the devil. Never found a trace. Their tracks led into a thicket and disappeared. Never saw hide nor hair of them again. Might have run off into thin air. Schneider, the Dutch-man who was with us, went up to Islamahad last week to report the business to the authorities. It was bloody strange—"

"I say!" Bradshaw got to his feet. "Th' mail boat's in, and there comes Schneider now. Look' at him run. He's all excited. Hey!" he called to the fat man pounding, unexpected, up the path. "What's up? You look like you'd seen one of our famous ghosts—"

The fat one puffed to the verandah; dropped cursing into a chair. Bradshaw, Fenway and Carter offered oaths of surprise. The Dutchman gulped down four drinks before he spoke. Then *"Dunder!* See a ghost, eh? So I did! I came to tell you. It was three days ago, in Malangore, on the way back. I was down at the bazaar. *Ach!* A beggar stopped me for alms. Stuck out a big dirty paw and gabbled for baksheesh. Never in my life haff I seen so wretched a looking man. Barefoot. Sunburnt. Red with fever. Just a big poisoned tramp. So. He was crazy, too. Lotus flowers stuck behind his ears. And do you know what he wass singing to himself? No, you wouldn't. But that crazy one wass singing to himself a Buddhist chant. It froze me right down to my heels when I heard it. You guess it did. And then this singing stopped and the crazy one was mumbling: 'I *saw* it! The Buddha. I saw, and I follow. I follow to Nirvana. For Buddha, the Eight-fold Way—' *Gott!* I yelled in his face, but he jumped like a jack-rabbit and bounced away in the mob. Then I got away, myself, I can tell you. Fast, for I was sick. But I haff one good look. There he wass, big with stiff red hair and beard and bright blue eyes. And on his temple a scar shaped like the letter Z—"

Carter and Fenway swore. The Dutchman echoed the word. "*Gott!* And it wass awful, yes. You remember, Bradshaw? You recall? 'Seeing,' he said, 'is believing!' *Ja.* And he saw—"

The naturalist nodded. Beyond the compound fence the smothered jungle murmured. The coal fell from his kalabash and the ashes scattered noisily on the floor.

# ABOUT THE AUTHOR

**AS A GUEST** speaker at Pulpcon in Dayton, Ohio in July, 1986, I played the old Q. and A. game. I believe the opening of that game makes a good beginning for the present discussion of my fiction writing for the pulps.

Q. How and when did my fiction writing begin?

A. I have in my files the initial effort—a book entitled *The Devul and the Knîght* [sic] written age five, hand-printed, hand-illustrated and hand-bound, price one cent (two copies, one remainder). The "K" circumflexed over the "night" was inserted by a brother ten years my senior. From the penny profit (from a sale within the family), I purchased a Mary Jane—taffy wrapped around a glob of peanut butter. Um.

Q. Then?

A. Shortly thereafter, I wrote, hand-printed, hand illustrated and hand-bound *Hawk Eye the Indian Boy* (two copies, price one cent, one remainder) which bought me another Mary Jane.

Q. And?

A. There followed a production entitled *The Sheriff of Red Roach Ranch*. ("Roach" was the spelling of my wicked older brother when I asked him if "Rock" was spelled with two "Ks." No matter.) I copied the spelling "Sheriff and "Ranch" from a book I was reading. Again, the one cent sale (leaving one remainder) paid for another Mary Jane.

Thus I conceived a notion.

Born was the idea that by writing I could eat.

That idea served as an apothegm for my subsequent career as a writer—a ruling not invariably a truism. As it eventuated there were times when I had Thanksgiving dinner at bottom of the totem pole at a hot dog stand.

However, I wrote many yarns for my high school magazine-an effort that caused an English teacher to suggest I submit a fiction effort to a magazine.

*Theodore Roscoe*

Not overly optimistic, I knew I couldn't compete in a try for that day's top, the *Saturday Evening Post*. So I picked a pulp—*NorthWest Stories*. Luck! A check for $40.00! And a request for another story. This first story, "The Duel," would appear in the September 1926 issue.

That did it.

It was summertime, and I'd been a temporary P.O. employee peddling mail on a route on Long Island. With a high school buddy similarly employed, who shared room and board. And I had just carried a very heavy parcel-post package addressed to a "Tillie Tisswisser," 8,001 some local avenue at the end of the line. After lugging it an extra half mile, I discovered there was no such address. Belatedly suspicious, I pried open one corner of the package and exposed a cinder block. Which my pal had wrapped and mailed with a slew of cancelled stamps.

That would have done it if my check hadn't come that day with $40.00. "I quit! I just made a fortune!" I told them at the P.O. where I dumped the cinder block. (And I got even with my buddy by ducking out of our boarding house by letting my suitcase out of our bedroom window on a clothes line and leaving him stuck with the rent.)

Anyway, the $40.00 check started me on what eventuated as a career, writing for *Action Stories, Argosy, Short Stories* and

*Adventure,* for such astute editors as Jack Byrne, Don Moore and, after the war (World War II), Burroughs Mitchell and Bud Hart. Of whom I still see Bud Hart—the others no longer among those present.

World War II pretty much killed most of the now extinct pulps. From paper shortage? I can't say. But many pulp writers faded away during the war. Among them, one of the best. Frederick Faust ("Max Brand"). I'm not certain, but I believe he may have been killed at Anzio.

If one finds some astonishing names among the early pulp editors some of the writers are equally surprising. In the early *Argosy-All Story.* Mary Roberts Rinehart, Octavus Roy Cohen, Zane Gray, E. Phillips Oppenheim, John Buchan. (Buchan, who wrote "The Thirty-Nine Steps," became Governor-General of Canada.)

**ONE** of the questions often asked me is how did I happen to write about an old veteran yarn-spinner who spun yarns about his service in the French Foreign Legion. In North Africa back in the early '30s I encountered on a street in Casablanca this old-time Legionnaire with hashmarks up to his elbow. He agreed to talk over wine at a *brasserie.*

He didn't wear the classic old-time Legion uniform-the button-back blue overcoat, white trousers, blue cummerbund, heavy desert-boots called *brodequins.* He wore an old artilleryman's outfit. But the square-brim *kepi* with the gold torch insignia was Legion.

Questioning him in my limping French, and struggling to comprehend his metaphors, I got a *formidable* story. Aside from obvious hyperbole and manifest adjectives, some of it was perhaps true.

Here was my prototype for Thibaut Corday. Which, of course, wouldn't be his right name. You could enlist in the Legion under any name you chose, and since his right name was Hyacinth Rastagouch, he chose Corday for what is called a *nom de guerre.* Which became your official name as a "Stepson of France."

Meaning you couldn't be extradited for a crime committed elsewhere—a fact, it was said contributed to the enlistment of numerous criminals using an alias. Who knows?

Because Frenchmen can't enlist in the French Legion, I had Corday say he was a Belgian. Or was it a Swiss? Anyway, the teller of my story attributed to Corday good English, partly translated.

Since his yarns were obviously mixtures of fact and fiction, I never presumed they would be taken seriously by the reader. And was surprised when several critics wrote to tell me the military tactics in this or that Corday tale were hokum. They were so intended to sound.

Incidentally, some Legion veterans in New York voted me an honorary member of the Veterans of the French Foreign Legion.

Actually, I never saw the Legion in combat. At a Legion H.Q. back in Sidi Bel Abbes, I was querying one of the officers. Apparently he thought I was planning to enlist. He shook his head at me with the comment: *"Discipline terrible!"* They followed the old rule, *"March qu creve."* "March or die." If a Legionnaire fell out, exhausted, in a Sahara march, they sent a sharpshooter back to kill him, and spare him from torture by desert tribesmen. But the Legionnaires I saw in action weren't risking their lives.

In Europe back then there was a saying. When the English conquer a country they build a custom house. The Germans build a fort. The French build a road. Back then (the '30s) the Legionnaires I saw in action were covered with not-very-glamorous dust, wielding picks and shovels building a road. Some of them in barracks slept in cots with the cot-legs in cans filled with water, to defeat scorpions. Their pay, if I recall correctly, afforded them a daily bottle of *pinard* (cheap red wine). Nothing so intriguing, colorful and lively as in such novels as *Beau Geste*.

So don't join the French Foreign Legion today. You'd get a plain khaki uniform, and risk only being bored to death.

Still, you'd learn one thing. Watch them, if chance occurs, on parade in France or on TV. There's no military outfit anywhere that can out-march their particular step.

**ASIDE** from the Foreign Legion, I most enjoyed writing for *Action Stories* a series about an adventurer named Peter Scarlet. There were at least 14 Peter Scarlet stories, beginning with "Jungle Joker" in the May 1927 issue of *Action Stories*. Other favorites were a tale entitled "On Account of a Woman" (*Adventure*, January 1936) and a tale for *Argosy*, "The Voodoo Express" (October 10, 1931).

On another tack, I enjoyed writing a series for *Argosy* titled "Four Corners," which began with "He Took Richmond" in the June 5, 1937 issue of *Argosy*. These were adventures experienced by a youngster whose uncle was Sheriff in a small town about 100 miles from New York. One of the early Four Corners stories was "I Was the Kid With the Drum" (October 30, 1937)—a murder mystery. They used to have a kid aid the drummer by carrying in a parade the front end of a big base drum (guess where the body was concealed in a hurry by the murderer in this case). Of course, the drum seemed heavier than usual. And the drum-beat seemed more of a thump than the usual vibratory boom. The kid in the story didn't get it. But anyway the murderous drummer discovered he'd killed the wrong person.

In another "Four Corners" tale, I had a thief change his money into coins—loot he could bury in a well. Okay? But when he went back to safely get and spend this big bag of coins, he was trapped by the fact the silver dollars all bore the same date—the date of the robbery.

In one of my favorite Four Corners stories, "Frivolous Sal" (*Argosy*, July 17, 1937), the small town gentry were worried because it was rumored the young woman, so named (after a popular song), kept a diary. Fruitless efforts were made to get hold of it. In the end? Try to guess it.

I had a lot of fun writing "The Head," which appeared in *Short Stories*, December 10, 1932. As a stringer reporter, I had gone to Panama to investigate rumors of "White Indians" in the remote interior near the Colombian border. At a bar in Cristobal I asked the bar-keep if he'd heard of these Indians. Overhearing my query, a bar-fly character asked if I was interred in Jiboro Indians—the tribe that, through a mysterious process, boned, cured and somehow shrank human heads to the size of a baseball. (Origin of the term "head-shrinker" for a psychologist.) The bar-fly said he had one to sell, and produced what appeared to be a much-shrunken human head. As the Jiboro Indians actually beheaded their enemies and with incredible artsy-crafty skill created such curiosities, I was interested in the specimen handed me by the bar-fly. Ah! Only $300.00.

But the bartender, behind his hand, winked at me a negative signal. I didn't buy the head.

When the bar-fly indignantly took off with his allegedly shrunken head, the bartender advised me it was a fake, a monkey head fixed up to look human.

Later I saw an authentic shrunken head on display in another bar.

When World War II put an end to my pulp efforts, by good luck I sold *Only in New England*—a novel I'd intended for *Argosy*—to Scribner's. Surprisingly, it made the Literary Guild Book of the Month.

Thereafter, I wrote two Navy histories—*U.S. Submarine Operations, World War II* (1949) and *U.S. Destroyer Operations, World War II* (1953) which were published by the Naval Institute at Annapolis (and are still on the market). I also wrote *This is Your Navy* (1950) for service reading. This was followed by *The Web of Conspiracy* (1959), about the Lincoln assassination, which became a *DuPont Show of the Month* on TV in 1961. Of which, with a great deal of help from my devoted wife, Rosamond, got me going again in fiction.

Today I can't recall what some of these tall tales written 50 years ago were about. Maybe I should have written some of them under an assumed name. But when I wrote them I felt I should take my lumps if, compared to many of early *Argosy's* great writers, my efforts proved mediocre. And on the other hand, if some drew plaudits, I'd like to take a bow in person.

Brave, no?

# THE ARGOSY LIBRARY ™

SERIES 4 INCLUDES:

* TUTTLE * ENGLAND * FARLEY *

* BRAND * BRENT * ROSCOE *

* GIESY & SMITH *

* RUD * PETTEE *

* CUNNINGHAM *

THE BEST FICTION
FROM THE FRANK
A. MUNSEY LINE

www.ingramcontent.com/pod-product-compliance
Lightning Source LLC
Chambersburg PA
CBHW030521020726
47494CB00004B/1183